ISLE OF YOU
A VISITOR'S GUIDE

Sam Sobelman

For every body with a burning heart,
A flame trapped within your chest.
You should probably get that looked at by a
trained professional.

ISLE OF YOU
A VISITOR'S GUIDE

RISE

Sun-scorched and well-cured, I woke on an unfamiliar shore under unfamiliar skies. My senses flooded my brain with uncertainty. I wouldn't have bet a dollar on which grainy beach I had washed onto, let alone who I was supposed to be. The salty ocean waters had smoothed my mind like a pebble until only a well-worn sense of self remained.

I opened my mouth and spewed a sinister conglomeration of seawater and sandy bits. The mixture scraped my throat as it rushed to freedom. Tiny crystals stuck to my tongue as I continued to vomit dry air. My nose was jammed, packed with beach particulate. The muddy brick walls in my nostrils disintegrated when I unleashed a quick sneeze.

Next on my agenda was finding my limbs. I couldn't feel a thing where I thought they might be attached to my body. My propioception was totaled, but I willed myself to motion, like a deaf conductor leading an orchestra of blind musicians. My fingers tingled somewhere off to my sides. They lay trapped under moist blankets of beach.

I flexed and flexed, with all my might, until strength returned to my hands. I kept willing myself to life, piece by piece. I reanimated my arms, my legs, my feet, and my torso. All my parts worked in tandem, combining their powers, to dig my body out of the grimy tomb where it lay buried. Finally, my corpse fully undead, I flipped myself onto my back and opened my sand-locked eyes.

The sky was aflame in a riot of colors. Golden ambers clashed with murky blues in a battle of attrition. My vision was the clear winner. The sun idled on the edge of the horizon, dangling its fiery gams off the edge of the world. I was unsure whether the golden sphere was coming or going, but the cool sand beneath my back gave me hope it was the former.

Vestiges of constellations lingered in the sky, but nothing about this starscape was familiar. I found no swans, no scorpions, and no ladles of cosmic soup. Searching for such strange icons in the sky seemed like a rather strange habit. Swans and scorpions could not survive in such thin atmosphere. I wasn't sure why I kept searching. The fact that my constellations were absent upset my spiritual navigation.

There wasn't a soul in sight or sound, but I sensed I was not alone in this strange place. The land literally throbbed with life. A pulse traveled through the well-packed sands, vibrating my weary bones. It drove me to stand and move, beating a native rhythm in my foreign heart.

Gazing inland, I saw topography unlike any I had ever imagined, in my dozen minutes of consciousness. A bright blue mountain penetrated the sky, tearing a scandalous hole through a veil of serpentine clouds. The base of the peak transformed into flamboyantly purple crags. A lush forest crawled up to the foot of the cliffs, tickling their toes with foliage. Hundreds of varieties of trees, ferns, and bushes grew together in harmony. Their leaves straddled the color spectrum, creating

2

a thick mosaic of aqua, emerald, ruby, and more colors my eyes were not prepared to process.

Amidst this verdant festival of life, a crooning dirge tickled the back of my neck. Something felt wrong. The beauty was too pristine, too perfect. It was almost unreal. I couldn't figure it out. Not knowing the source of this unease started to gnaw at me; I worried something else might want to gnaw at me.

A thick, sepia mist adorned the mountain and permeated the forest with probing tendrils. The land was playing a tease, wearing the mist as a shifting slip, hinting at what lay beneath but not giving it all away. It wanted to seduce me, urged me to enter more deeply. The rising warmth behind me told me that the mist would soon burn away, but I did not trust myself to return from a journey into the forest at this moment. There was little chance she would let me leave.

I choked down my land-lust and listened to the rhythm of the sand instead. The beat drew my focus out of the forest and carried me along the beach. I moved down the shore, every single step a rediscovery of my body. I swore that some devil had snapped off my original limbs and attached a new pair from a rag doll. My feet felt the vibrations between every grain of sand as they ground against each other between my toes. The pulsing waves made their way up into my belly and I realized the depths of my hunger.

An awareness of my stomach appeared out of nowhere, like a long-lost child begging for donations. I looked down to see a tiny gut, slightly distended. The ripples of its desire spread through my body. Its desperation manifested as unbearable pain and upset growls. I doubled over, falling to my tender knees.

Food had become of utmost priority. But what could I eat? What was a thing like me supposed eat in a place like this?

A second wind lifted my legs and wrapped them in jet streams, as the pulse of the earth intensified. In the distance, I could see a small brown blip on the seashore. A small pier partway between us indicated the blip might be inhabited. I dragged myself onward, never quite running, never quite falling.

The brown house loomed ever closer, subliming into the shape of a beach hut. Weather-beaten and rickety, it looked little more than an outhouse, much less a house for anyone to inhabit. As I passed the pier, I noticed it was far down the path of rot. The beams supporting the end of the pier had collapsed, dipping it into the sea. It had been abandoned long ago. I feared the shack would be just as desolate. When I arrived, I knocked on the shabby door, taking care not to collapse the whole structure with my might.

"Hello, is anybody home?" I asked, my voice swallowed by the porous wood. I waited for several minutes, but heard no reply.

Mustering all the courage my waterlogged body could manage, I grabbed the door handle and pushed the entrance open. The interior of this humble hut shocked my eyes dry.

The inside of the shack belonged to a much grander quarter than the outside implied. My subconscious shorted out trying to fit the largeness of the room inside the tininess of the shack, but my attention was otherwise occupied. Three walls stood lined with shelves from ceiling to floor, packed with loads of odds and ends. Books, bottles, and bouncing bears, each claimed a third of the room. The fourth wall, opposite the threshold, was equipped with a grand, brick fireplace, gently illuminating the room. A table at the center of the space was covered in a holey, maroon tablecloth. A great wooden chair with fell beasts engraved on its arms and legs sat open to the table. The miracle that all of this stuff was able to fit inside an outhouse was lost on me.

The only sight for my eyes was the bowl of ripe fruit sitting stoically in the center of the table. My mouth flooded like a clogged bathtub and my stomach churned, begging me to act. Without pausing to think, I lunged at the table and began stuffing my face with juicy fruit-flesh.

The fruits appeared strange to my eyes, but they erupted with ecstasy on my tongue. Layers of flavors spilled their stories down my gullet, abating my stomach's pain with charming delicacy. I swallowed four, five, six fruit in half as many minutes, devouring their seeds and stems without a second thought. My teeth rent their flesh indiscriminately. Orange, cyan, silver, and viridian

5

juices flowed from my lips. A culinary rainbow mixed in my gut.

I gulped and glutted until the bowl was empty. Sated, my stomach began to relax. I looked down to find it had swelled far beyond its previous size. My skin shined bright, reflecting my inner happiness. Also, it was covered in many milliliters of fruit juice. As my thoughts peeled away from vanquished food, a sobering crash brought me to my feet.

I leapt from the chair and spun, lurching out of control. The doorway harbored a monstrous shadow, buttressed by flares of light from the rising sun. Horrible thoughts vibrated my core, threatening to jiggle me apart. Instead, they just waggled my tongue.

"A beast of the darkness has risen from the ocean's depths, determined to drag me back beneath the ocean waves! This is not acceptable! I'm too young to die! I've lived but a few minutes of life!"

I grabbed the only weapon within reach, the empty fruit bowl.

"Stay back, ocean monster! You will not drown me again!"

"Oh, stop that silliness, young thing. Harrumph!" the shadow bellowed. "I'd have eaten you already if I'd had a mind to."

The shadow stepped forward, dragging its mass through the doorframe. As its face came into the smooth hearth-light, the monster's terrible identity was revealed.

A sharp beak protruded from a mass of sunburned, pink flesh that was supposed to be some kind of head. It looked more like a thick mound of putty that had been chewed and partially digested, with two devilish, red eyes buried in the thick of it. The blob attached via a long, flabby neck to a humongous body covered in black feathers. Two epic wings stretched wide, as though they hadn't been used in years. A pair of elephantine talons, scaly and dry, supported the entire mass of the monster's body.

Dubious of the creature's words, I raised my bowl in defense.

"Stop your trickery now, sea- err, sky devil! I'm terribly gamy and not very delicious. I think. Actually, I don't know how delicious I am, but I'll be damned if I let you find out!"

"Oh, stop it already. Didn't you hear me?" The great avian shuffled around me and made his way to the hearth. "Harrumph! The least you could have done is put another log on the fire. Children these days, no respect!"

He lifted a log from a pile in the corner of the room and placed it into the fire. Sparks danced and a plume of smoke wiggled its way up the shack to a pinhole chimney in the roof. For such a small hole, it sucked fumes away efficiently.

"I'm sorry," I said, "I didn't notice the logs there until now."

The bird shook his head. "Please, don't worry about it. This is my home, after all. I do know all its tics and tacs. I can't expect a stranger to work his way around without making a few mistakes, here and there. Harrumph! My, those rumblies disappeared mighty quickly. Do you know anything about that?"

I dropped my defensive stance. "I'm so sorry. I didn't even think about what I was doing. I was so hungry; I never stopped to ponder the consequences. Please forgive me."

The bird shook his bulbous head, jiggling his neck flab. "It's fine, it's fine. I always welcome company. The shore can surely be a lonely place sometimes. The name's Hammond, by the way. What's yours?"

I nodded and placed the bowl back on the table. "Nice to meet you, Hammond. I'm not sure what my name is, to tell the truth."

Hammond's red eyes bulged. "What? Harrumph! You can't even remember your name? That's unfortunate. A true tragedy. Whatever shall I call you? Do you remember anything at all?"

"Not specifically. I have no clue who I am or where I come from. My brain is real beat up. I mean, some things make sense to me. I've got my words, when I need them. Most of the time. I think. I don't know, they just come out right. Maybe I've got them all backwards. I really don't know what I know. Whether it's the truth or something that I made up. But, any sort of facts or names are impossible to place."

Hammond bobbed his cranium. "Harrumph! Conditional amnesia, oh, I've heard of this before. How did you get to the island, little earthbound beast?"

"I washed up on the shore, pure as though I'd just been born."

Hammond wiggled his corpulence in a dance of joy. "Yes! I knew it. This happens to all the beasts that come in through the ocean passage. There must be something in the water, yes! Harrumph! That must be it!"

"Um, Hammond, I'm a bit confused. How did you get here?"

"Well, I flew here, of course. Look at these!" He spread his wings wide. "These are the wings of a beautiful creature. Aren't you envious, little wingless one?"

"Of course, my brain must still be waterlogged. Does that mean you could fly away? Back to wherever you came from?"

"Yes," Hammond agreed, "I suppose it does. However, I'm not so sure where that place is. Harrumph! Or, I suppose, if I would even want to go back. This is quite the pleasant island. And I'm living in a most luxurious flat, if I do say so myself."

"Does it have a name? The island, I mean."

"It has many different names, depending on who you ask. I like to call it the Roundabout. I've heard it called New Bonia, which is a bit silly, and the Last Resort, but that's just ridiculous. Ah, well, nobody values the opinions of an old fart like me anymore. Harrumph! Everyone's got his or her own take on it. Everyone's a critic! Harrumph!"

"So, it doesn't have a proper name?"

"Not that I know of."

"Isn't that a little bit weird."

"Well, you don't have a name either. Are you weird, too?"

"Sure," I nodded, unsure whether the bird was being sarcastic. "So, there are other people on this island? Err, other creatures."

"Of course! What kind of backwater atoll do you think this is? Some folks wash up on the shore, just like you. Harrumph! Some folks come from the sky, like me. They're all scattered about, the island. Apparently, I'm the only fellow who can't get enough of the shore."

"Why's that?"

"I guess I'm just that type of bird."

"And, what kind of bird is that?" I asked, a slight tickle trickling down my throat.

His ruby eyes glinted with pride. "I, good lad, am an egress, keeper of knowledge and tender of mini-bears."

"An egress? Really? No, that doesn't feel right." The tickle turned into a full-on itch. "You're something else, something less glamorous."

Hammond placed the mid of his wings where his hips might have gone. "Oh, well, if you know what kind of bird I am, please tell me. And why bother asking me? Harrumph! You don't even know your name, but suddenly you're a master ornithologist?"

"No, I didn't mean that. It's just that, when I think of an egress, I don't think of you."

"Well, that's a whole lot clearer, young man. Whatever you might think of an egress where you're from, it doesn't apply here. I am an egress of this island, and that is all that matters. You'd do well never to forget that Rule."

It didn't feel right. I didn't know why. This place was operating under rules that I just couldn't grasp.

"I guess I'll have to take your word for it," I said, "Are there other folks like you on this island? Other egresses?"

"Oh sure, I talk to them all the time. Me and the other egresses, we flock together like birds of a feather. Is that what you want to hear? Harrumph! No, boy. That's highly offensive and supremely racist of you. Don't just assume things about other folk based on the color of their down. That's how prejudice gets born and spread! So ignorant! Harrumph! Today's youth!"

"I'm sorry, I didn't mean anything by it. I just wanted to know if there are any other people on the island."

11

"Oh, you mean people like you? Other little naked racists?"

It hadn't occurred to me before that moment, but I had spent the entire day in the nude. The ocean had swallowed my clothes, but had spit me out due to my disgusting flavor. I knew I tasted bad! I covered myself with the empty fruit bowl as my cheeks flushed.

"I'm so sorry. I didn't mean to be rude."

Hammond seemed puzzled by my words. "Don't be so uptight, boy. I'm merely teasing. It's not like I'm wearing any pants. Don't think I give a squawk."

I noted this fact and tried to keep my eyes on his pudgy face. I didn't even want to imagine the nether regions of this monster. "That is true, but I'm still a bit embarrassed."

The bird nodded. "Don't worry about it. The other little racist I met was the same way, for a while. I guess it takes a while to get used to our island ways." He shuffled over to a shelf of stuffed bears and took one down, a male cub.

"Wait a second. You mean there are others like me here? Other humans?"

Hammond turned and dropped a pile of clothing on the table. "Put those on. And no, I don't mean there are others of your kind here. Wingless folk don't seem to stick around on the island too long. Harrumph. There was one like you, a long time ago. He gave me those clothes for my mini-bear collection. Said he wanted me to remember him forever. I suppose it's appropriate if I let you remember him for a little while and I take a break from my duties."

"Where is he now?"

The bird shrugged. "He made a raft and took off on a quest for adventure. He disappeared over the horizon, last I saw. Took himself and his hairy, bigot body far, far away."

I slipped on the clothing while the bird related his tale. He had given me a green, leather jacket with bright purple pants; they fit me like my own skin. Could it be? "He disappeared into the sea? He didn't happen to look like me, did he?"

Hammond shook his head. "No, not a tic. Harrumph! He was a big, dark, muscular chap with sandy golden hair and a well-sprouted chest. He was nothing like you, shrimp. Harrumph! I bet you couldn't even lift the wood he used to make his raft."

"But, if he's so much bigger than me, why do his clothes fit me perfectly?"

The bird shook his head. "Must be the salty sea air, shrinking them down. It does that, you know. It's been years since that boy left. I haven't heard a peep from him since." I prodded him a bit more, but that was all Hammond would say about the matter of the boy or his raft.

"Well, Hammond, I'm grateful for your hospitality. I don't feel welcome taking all this charity without offering you anything in return. I ate all your food and I'm wearing your bear's stylish outfit. Surely, there must be something I can do to repay you."

Hammond's beak popped open wide. "Ah, yes! My fruit! I'd completely forgotten! Harrumph! You ate every single one. Now that you mention it, I'm quite famished." His crimson eyes flared and his serrated beak smacked. "Yes, I think that would be the perfect task for you. Go refill my bowl with fruit from the grove out back. That's not too hard, right? It's just a short way into the forest."

I nodded; this seemed more than fair. "Just straight into the forest?"

"Yep, that's right. Just a few hundred yards. You'll be there before you know it."

"A few hundred yards! That's hardly a short ways. I'll get lost, for certain."

"Harrumph!" Hammond sighed. "No, you won't. There's a path that some folk use. Just be sure to make it back by sundown and you should be fine. It's a straight walk I promise."

I felt less than sure of my companion's intent. "Do you promise? You swear on your life that it's safe?"

The giant bird made some noise that resembled laughter, but was more like pebbles being tossed about a laundry machine. "I promise. But do be careful of the mists. Bad things lurk in the mists, if you catch my drift. Harrumph! Make it a point to get back here by nightfall and you'll have no trouble."

He flexed his beak into a smile. "No trouble at all."

SHINE

Hammond lent me a machete to cut myself a path if the roughage grew too thick.

"Do you know how thick it grows? Will I need this?" I asked. "I've never used a blade before, as far as I remember."

"No, boy. Harrumph! I don't know how thick it grows. I always fly there directly whenever I go! It's about a five-minute flight! I think."

"Only five minutes as the egress flies! That's fine, but it will take me ages to get there on my own!"

"Maybe so. It would be a lot simpler if you had a pair of wings," the old bird admitted. "But, since you have to go through the woods, you'd best hurry if you want to get back before darkness falls. Scuttle off while Hammond takes a nap, little git. Harrumph!"

Something about the bird's cheery attitude left me feeling less than confident. But, I owed him. No matter Hammond's intention, he was hospitable and I always paid my debts. At least, I would try my damnedest to pay my first debt of this conscious life.

By the time I left for the fruit grove, the sun was high in the sky, beating the earth with its sledgehammer heat. I dashed a short way across the open sand to the sheltering trees, sweat dripping down my neck faster than I could wipe it away.

Thankfully, the strange jacket I had adorned was well designed for hot weather. The leather was treated to breathe and a cooling breeze was able to sneak in beneath the hemline.

As I expected, the mists had burned away, leaving the forest bright and inviting. A gaping maw in the foliage called to me, indicating the start of my path. I plunged into the vegetable realm, carrying the large bowl in front of me to clear a path and protect myself from rogue branches. Whip-like limbs slapped against my shield, eager to scratch up my brand new style.

Despite my initial misgivings, the trek began without any issues. At one time, this path had been well used. The surrounding vegetation appeared to respect the trail's sanctity; the way was clear of overgrowth. I wondered if the fruit of this garden was a major food source for the island. Perhaps, for the island's herbivores? I hoped that vegetarianism was the most popular lifestyle!

I traveled deep into the forest, counting away the yards by my paces. At two hundred yards, my energy flared. No distance was too great for me to surmount. After four hundred yards, my fire was stoked but beginning to wane. The mouth of the path was still marked behind me by a tiny, shining portal. Near six hundred yards, my embers sputtered. Even flying above the trees, Hammond shouldn't have been able to make this trek in only a few minutes. There was no end to the path in sight. The egress hadn't told me the whole truth about these woods.

After I counted eight hundred yards, I glanced over my shoulder again. The path stretched behind me into darkness; the entrance had disappeared some minutes ago while I was distracted by strange shadow patterns in the foliage. I panicked and lost myself. A strange driver grabbed my thought-reins as the pulse from the earth returned, whipping me into action.

I had forgotten about the beats. Rather, I thought they had disappeared my rapacious hunger had been sated. The throbbing returned with a vengeance, spurring my ass forward and the rest of me with it. I sprinted as fast as I could, unthinking. Whether I moved away from or toward the source of the rhythm, I couldn't have guessed. I ran like a robot, programmed with a single, prime directive: run. I held the bowl before me like a ramming shield and plunged through the forest blindly. The machete bounced at my side, as useful as a hammer in a laser duel.

Without warning, I emerged from the dark path into an open, sunny realm. My eyes overloaded, blinded by pure energy flowing from the heart of the woods. Momentum carried me forward, toward the source of light, and a scene from a tapestry materialized before my eyes. In the center of an emerald orchard, sat a porcelain fairy that sapped my strength without so much as an awkward glance. She set some sorcery over me to pin my feet to the ground, freeze my arms in place, and halt my every breath. She was enchanting.

The girl sat cross-legged on a soft lawn, light filtering through the treetops to glint off of her pink, gossamer locks. Dozens of polygonal wisps darted about the space above her head, leaving rose, gold, and blue streamers in their wake. The white of her sundress looked tan against her skin. Its torso was painted every color I could name and then some, stained proudly by juices dripping from fruits in her hands. These delicacies had been plucked off branches of the scores of trees around her, each tree bearing a fruit with uniquely patterned skin. Unfinished rinds littered the crisp grass around her subtle bottom. She moved one delicate finger to her lips, wiping a drip of sparkling nectar into her mouth.

Suddenly, the bewitching dryad acknowledged my presence and the spell was broken.

"Oh, hello there! Won't you come sit with me and have a bite or two?"

I stumbled and stuttered as I made my way toward to the girl. Of all things, she had stolen my ability to speak!

"That's quite the lovely bowl you've got there," she continued, "Where'd you get it? A thrift store somewhere? A vintage shop, perhaps? Or is it a family heirloom?"

Still unable to speak in complete words, I fought the nymph's spell with all the will I could muster. I muttered something along the lines of "Mmmrrrmmhhh."

The girl laughed, filling the air with a sweet tinkle of bells mixed with the rasp of warm laundry.

I felt vestiges of her charm grip me tighter with each of her shining chuckles. "Gosh, you can't even talk! Are you mute? Deaf? Blind? Do you lack a sense of smell? I always forget what that one is called. How did you manage to get yourself all the way to my secret grove, silly boy?"

"I just, well, huh," I mumbled, heat filling my cheeks, "I just followed the path. It was more or less straightforward. Straight forward to you."

The girl blinked. "Which path is that?"

"The path right behind me. The one that I came from. Can't you see it?"

I turned about to find the path had disappeared. In its place was a turquoise shrubbery with magenta berries. There was no sign that I had just moments ago burst into the clearing, running for my life. Thinking that the plants must have just snapped back into place, I plunged my head into the shrub, looking for any evidence of my path. There was nothing. The forest had swallowed everything.

"All I see is that plummery bush," the girl replied. "Don't eat those berries, they're poisonous. I tried one and vomited almost immediately. But, they are just as delicious as they look. So, go right ahead, if you think it's worth the risk. I think you'd be better off coming over and eating some rumblies with me, instead. I just can't stop myself from devouring every single one that I lay a finger on. They're perfectly safe and are jam packed with awesome flavor. It's savory but sweet! It's naturally salty, yet refreshing as a breeze. It's a real trip, man!"

Confounding confusion mixed with remnants of the girl's spell and meddled in my thoughts. I stumbled over and sat down beside the girl. It was the only thing I could think to do without thinking. "Ah, I see. Well, miss…"

"Please, call me Vespa."

"Ah, ok, Vespa. Well, I need to ask you something a little bit strange."

"A strange query on a first date? What a scandal! But, aren't you going to at least tell me your name first?"

I blushed. "I'm not sure what to tell you. I don't know my name, or even if I ever had one."

Vespa dropped her jaw. "What do you mean? That's terrible! You must have a name!"

"I don't! I lost my memory when I woke on this island. I washed up on the beach. The first thing that I remember is spitting sand and salty water out of my mouth and looking up at the sky. I didn't have any clothes or clues as to who I am or who I used to be."

"Really? You just came out of the ocean? You got spit up by the big blue baby?"

"A baby?"

"Well, sure! The ocean is always waving hello and goodbye. It's constantly swallowing things it shouldn't and wetting itself all over. Sounds like a baby to me."

"I suppose, so. But still, why? Is it so odd that a baby spat me up? I'm pretty sure I taste terrible."

"I think you mean to say you have terrible taste. Look at those pants!"

"Well, sheesh! It's not like I had a huge wardrobe to change into. How did you get here, anyway? Wait, are you a native?"

"Ha! No, silly, do I look like a native?"

I shrugged, unsure of what a native was supposed to look like.

"No, I fell out of an airplane," Vespa continued.

"You must be joking! You got spat out by a big baby in the sky?"

"Don't be smart! No, sir. I was traveling with my parents during winter vacation and, all of a sudden, the emergency exits opened up. Every single one! I got sucked out of my seat, as did my parents, a bunch of other folks, and all the luggage. Now I understand why they have those seatbelt lights, I guess. That's the last thing I remember, looking at that stupid light while I was being tossed about like a rag doll. Next thing I knew, I found myself here, alone."

"You fell right here? In this glen?"

Vespa nodded.

"What about the others, did they land nearby?"

"I suppose." Vespa shrugged. "I haven't heard a peep from any of them since I got here. I'm not sure what happened exactly, but I'm pretty sure we got separated during the fall."

"Oh, yes, they're probably fine. I hear a lot of creatures come in from the sky. How long has it been since you arrived?"

Vespa began to count on her fingers. "Oh, must be eight or nine days. I've explored this grove pretty thoroughly, but the food is so delicious! I can't leave! I don't really feel a need to traipse about so I can get lost when I've got plenty of rumblies right here. I may as well stay in one spot until my family or one of the other passengers comes to find me. It is disgustingly comfortable, sitting on the grass all day, feasting non-stop. Though, I'm glad to have some company at last."

"What about your luggage?" I asked, coughing away the hot emotion rushing to my brain.

She shook her head. "Not a trace. I've been wearing the same underpants for over a week! I should just go without."

I blushed hard, turning rosier as Vespa's grin spread wider.

"What a glamorous life, the island life," I choked.

"Really now, at least falling from forty thousand feet is a sight more fashionable than washing up on the seashore with kelp and jellyfish in my hair. That's just gross. Speaking of gross, we can't have you without a name. I just won't stand for it! How do you like Hammond?"

"Hammond? What an odd coincidence. I just met a big bird named Hammond. I don't think that I'm much of a Hammond type."

"You're absolutely right. It's also my favorite cousin's name. Yes, Hammond's a much too common name for an exemplary bloke like you. How about Charlie?"

Another of Vespa's spells hit me right then, square in the chest. "That's perfect. I love it." I wasn't sure what kind of magic she was casting over me, but I didn't care too much. I was sure she could use nothing but the good kind.

Vespa squealed with laughter and clapped. "Whatever your name used to be, it doesn't matter anymore. You will always be Charlie to me. Do you feel me?"

"I feel you," I smiled, imagining what it would be like to actually feel her. "I could get used to that."

As long as she you're the one calling me, I added, to myself.

Vespa poked me in the shoulder. "So Chaaarlieee," she stretched out the pronunciation of my name, savoring each syllable, "Didn't you have a question for me?"

"Oh, right!" I said, scrambling to regain my thoughts, "I wanted to ask if you had seen any others like us on the island, but you sort of answered me already. It wasn't the answer I was hoping for, but the truth is the truth. There might be people here, somewhere, but even they probably won't know how to get off the island. And, well, the truth is that I was hoping that maybe someone like us could help me regain some of my memories."

"Memories are overrated. Live for the present, Charlie," Vespa said, shooing the thoughts away. "I haven't met any other humans on the island. In fact, I've only seen birds and bees since I've been here."

"Really? What about this orchard? Surely, someone or someones has to come here to tend it? Have you seen them?"

Vespa shrugged, irritated by my lack of common sense. "The birds and the bees see to that, obviously."

"That's too bad. I was hoping someone could help me out. I feel so stranded and lost."

"How delightfully angsty. Why don't you sing me a song about it?" Vespa sighed. "No, please don't. Look, if you're really stuck on that thought, I could tell you about where I come from. Maybe it'll jog some memories loose inside that soggy head of yours."

"Yes! Let's do that. You just might be on to something."

"While we're at it, why don't you fill up that bowl of yours with some more fruits for me. I'm getting hungry again."

"But you ate so many already!" I said, "They must not have been very filling."

A silver-blue rind bounced off my forehead, an excellent shot by the pixie girl. "Here's an important fact about where I'm from: girls don't like it when you imply they're fat."

As I gathered fruit from surrounding trees, Vespa related to me tales of her home.

"I come from an urban center, a hub to the bustling world-at-large. There, buildings rise higher than the mountains on the island. You can't walk two feet without bumping into another human being. It's not like here, where we are truly unique. There are just masses and masses of unwashed masses, everywhere. But, I was basically one of the royalty in this metropolis, living life on top of the heap. Power flowed from my family's fingertips and wealth from our toes. Celebrities and commoners the world over constantly requested our presence at all their parties. Oh, the parties! Endless fountains of food and drink! Non-stop musical festivals for weeks at a time. Oh, and the armies of robot slaves! They could do anything! It was really swell, living life at the top of the world. We were incredibly famous, for some reason."

"You don't remember why these so-called celebrities called you?"

"I don't know. They probably just fell in love with my girlish wiles and my feminine wit. My memory's a little skuzzy, all right? I probably bumped something when I fell forty thousand feet, remember?"

"I suppose. It's just that, well, how can you be sure your influence was so strong if you don't know why you were famous?"

"Look, I just know that I'm an important figure! One of the elite members of society! And-"

"And all those unnecessarily large buildings! The glamorous lifestyle! The money! Well, it all seems a little bit excessive, don't you think? Why are there so many shallow, grandiose gestures where you are from? Honestly, this simple island does right by me. There's nothing too strange here, as far as I can tell."

"That world seems strange to you? Come on, you were probably born in one of the skyscrapers, lived in one of the skyscrapers, and would have died in one of the skyscrapers if you hadn't been swept away to this place. For all you know, you got sucked out of the very same plane I was riding."

"I don't know what to tell you," I said, "But that sort of life is just a bit too peculiar for me to believe."

"Really? Well, why don't you tell me a little bit about your hometown, Charlie? Think you can dredge something out of that garbage bin brain of yours?"

As she wished, I told her stories. However, I lacked any real memories of home, so I created a world of fictions using nothing but my rambling imagination.

"There are many things to fear where I come from, but nothing more-so than the Steel Corsairs. They ride their flying pirate ships through the skies, attacking steel barons and capturing wayward maidens. They claim to be furthering the cause of justice. In reality, they are just radical punks with no sense of home, with broken moral compasses."

"Oh, come on. That's a steampunk world, guy. It didn't happen. Get over it already. You can't lie to me, okay? I won't have it."

I shrugged her remark away. "Well, you can't blame this guy for trying." Being with her made me talk differently, possibly a lingering effect from her spell. I wanted to ask her what kind of magic she had used on me, but I wasn't comfortable broaching the subject.

We sat around in silence for a while after that, gobbling up the fruit I had gathered. I tried a green sphere with red stars spotting its skin. It was just as delicious as the fruits I had eaten earlier, but filled me with yet another unique flavor. Vespa watched me eat with a sly grin. I blushed a brighter pink than the juice dribbling down my chin, staining my shirt.

"So, your hometown," I started, "Do you think there's anyway that I could have come from there?"

Vespa's reply was accompanied by a sidelong glance. "Not in those clothes you couldn't. You look like a sick pony. In my hometown, you would have probably been put down by now."

"Oh! These aren't mine. They belong to a friend. The big egress, Hammond, he said they were given to him by a boy who visited the island before."

"Another boy? Here? Why didn't you track him down to help your sorry self? He probably knows how to deal with your man-issues better than I do."

"I would have tried, but he left a long time ago."

Vespa lunged at me faster than I could think. She pinned my arms to my sides. "He got off this rock? You've got to tell me how he did it. Let's go together; we'll escape back to my home. I'm sure we can find you a different outfit once we're there."

"It's quite simple. He built himself a raft and disappeared into the sea. We could probably do something like that, if we gathered some supplies."

"Are you joking?" Vespa's face melted into a frown and she let me go. "That's disastrous, damn it. Never mind. I can't swim. Damn! It's too risky. I'm not ready to face that challenge. For now, let's take

29

our chances here and hope that someone comes looking for us."

"And if they don't?"

I received no reply. The pink-locked girl had clasped her lips.

A cold sensation whipped through my bones. This wasn't another ethereal invocation from Vespa, working its way through my system. It was the lonely gale of dusk's descent, settling in for the evening.

"Oh, I'm sorry. I didn't mean to upset you. Look, I need to get away from here, now. You do too! It's not safe out here at night. Besides, I promised Hammond I would have the fruit back by nightfall."

Vespa said nothing.

"I'm serious! You should come with me. Hammond knows a lot about the island. I'm sure he'll help us figure a way off this island once he sees how many rumblies we've picked. He's a good bird. Well, I think he is."

Without a word, Vespa kicked over my bowl, scattering its contents far and wide. I dropped to my knees, scrambling to grab as many as I could.

"Hey! What did you do that for?" I cried, scooping an armful of fruit back into the bowl.

My only response was a sultry whistle from the wind. When I turned to look around, Vespa was gone.

SET

    I scrambled to my feet as the last remaining color-wisps scattered to the sky. Their taffeta tails trailed off into the molten colors of the setting sun. Another chill breeze turned my bones to crystal and my blood to cream. Whatever his true intentions, Hammond's warning against the forest nights was beginning to ring true. I wanted to run back to the safety of the shore, but I couldn't just abandon the girl who had enchanted me so keenly.

    "Vespa!" I cried. "Come back! I'm sorry, for whatever I did. I didn't mean to upset you." My words reverberated through the vacant glen. "Come on, it's getting late. We've got to get out of here before darkness falls!" My calls elicited no response.

    Manic, I searched for an exit from the orchard. My feet propelled me around the perimeter but I couldn't find a trace of the path I had traveled into the garden. There was no sign of Vespa making her exit through the dense foliage, either.

    "Stay calm," I told myself. "This is a good sign. Vespa is probably still somewhere in the orchard, hiding from me for whatever reason. I might not remember much about girls or their whimsical wiles, but, really, who does?" I ran down each of the orchard's dozen rows, glancing around tree trunks and up in their branches, searching. No strange, girlish shapes hid among their leaves. No mysterious bulges stood half-concealed behind their trunks.

I was traveling up yet another column when I abruptly found my feet above my head. My spine snapped taut, cracking like a whip. The machete slipped from its scabbard at my waist and bounced hilt-first off my nose. It settled in the grass a few arm's lengths away from my radical inversion. My body dangled upside-down from a thin brown rope that slithered out of the foliage of a tree bespeckled by sienna rumblies. I swayed in a burgeoning wind as my senses recalibrated, adjusting to this change in perspective. I struggled against gravity, flexing and twisting my muscles until I reached my ensnared ankle. I was able to grab the rope with both hands, but it was impossible to untie. The cord seemed to writhe against my will, alive and aware.

A cramp ripped through my belly. This body was still too weak to fight for too long. Thoroughly exhausted by my efforts, I relaxed myself back into a dangling position to recover. The sky melted from golden dusk to frigid night while I played a helpless pendulum. There was no escaping the evening, anymore.

"Hello?" I shouted. "Vespa, if you're still here, this isn't funny. Come let me down!"

"Nope, it's not Vespa responsible for this situation," said a deep voice from the darkness. The voice's timbre was tinted with slurred melody, like a jazz bass line.

"Who's there?" I asked. "Are you the one who set this trap?" I looked about the dimming orchard, but I couldn't see anyone else.

"Yes, I am, little critter. I'm the greatest hunter on this here island and I trap for keeps. You belong to me, now."

"Well," I said, "Why don't you show yourself and get this over with? Whatever you're planning to do, just please make it fast. I'm in a hurry to find someone, so I'd appreciate it if you could just tell me what all this is about."

"Ha!" he replied. "No wonder you were such easy prey! Here I am, right below you and you haven't even noticed!"

I craned my neck to get a glimpse of my captor. On the ground below me was a small fuzzy ball of brown feathers with a long white beak. Its body was about the same size as my right thigh. Two black, beady eyes stared up at me from the lump of feathers that comprised its head. The creature bounced on a pair of oversized talons. I grinned. The bird was much too adorable to be threatening.

"You're the terrible creature that's captured me? But, you're so cute! How did I let that happen? Come on, untie me and let's play a game of snuggles!"

The bird pecked me on the forehead and bumbled away. His body did not appear to be evolved for grace. "I told you once, I'll tell you again. I'm the best hunter on this entire island. Don't you forget it!"

I shrugged, a much more difficult task when done while dangling upside-down. "So, what exactly happens now, master hunter? What are you going to do with me now that you've caught me? Shall we swap some stories over a rumbly pie? Oh, what's your favorite color rumbly? I personally like the purple with green speckles. It reminds me of, well, of something. I can't recall what."

The fat little bird danced about, hopping from one set of talons to the other. "Ahh, the possibilities are exciting, aren't they? I could sell you as a slave, but you don't quite have the right constitution. I couldn't get a very high price for an ugly, Wingless mess like you, no. I could eat you, I suppose, but you don't look particularly tasty. I'd rather eat a whole plate of these rumblies. Maybe I could have you make a rumbly pie. Oh, that might be one of the greatest ideas I've ever had! Now you see, I'm rather clever. It's how I try to catch all my prey. With wits!"

"Oh, but of course," I nodded, trying to keep my circulation flowing against gravity. My face was growing bloody warm.

"Most likely, what I'll do is make a trophy out of you! Yeah, those clothes'll look real nice once I have you taxidermied. Maybe I'll do it so I can pose you every day. Like a flighty, little ballerina! Or a terrifying warrior! I'll really attract the chicks if they think I'm brave, you know?"

"I suppose that makes sense," I replied, unable to fault his logic. "Women do like a gentleman who makes them feel safe. If I may ask, how are you going to kill me? I think a man deserves to know his fate."

"Well," the hunter replied, "I haven't really gotten that far. This is my first time, after all."

My heart dropped up out of my mouth and onto the ground. "Really, on your first time out hunting you catch me? I must have no natural survival skills at all."

"Oh, this isn't my first time out hunting, no sir," the bird replied, "It's just the first time I've actually caught anything!"

"That certainly doesn't make me feel any better. But, hold on a second, didn't you say that you are the best hunter on this island? That record doesn't really support your claim."

"Well, I never," the bird said, in a huff. "I'm the only hunter on this island, by professional choice. So, that makes me the best. The other hunters, they were born into that role. I chose to be a hunter, so, I don't really think of those beasts as hunters. Besides, they've got no class. We aren't friends, that's for sure. No, sir."

My body slowly spun as it dangled. The bird walked around as I twirled, keeping pace with my face. I looked up at the sky. The sun had vanished, leaving a matte bluish-black pasted across the heavens. No stars glittered in the sky that night, having abandoned us for heavenly pursuits. Downy's rope squeezed ever tighter around my ankle, so I decided to try my hand at a more subtle escape.

"Master hunter, if you don't mind, I've got a personal question for you."

The bird tilted his head to the side, turning an ear to my plea. "Okay, shoot away, my little Trophy."

"What kind of beast are you?"

"Are you joking? I'm a falcon!" The bird's feathers ruffled like a mahogany pincushion. "Haven't you ever seen a falcon before? We falcons are birds of prey. We ride the thermals until our quarry is caught. We swoop like fell beasts and soar like hernias."

"I just," I started. "I don't understand." I realized that the sooner I was able to accept this fact, the more likely I would survive the island. Memories of Hammond's cryptic warnings flickered through my skull. Night was tossing a heavy blanket upon us.

"There's nothing to understand," the falcon said, "Other than the fact that I am the best hunter around. That's all you need to get through your hairy little head."

"Are there other falcons on the island?"

My captor jumped away at my query. He hopped around my dangling self with a devilish fervor. "Hah! Other falcons. Other falcons!" The bird mumbled to himself as he wound circles tighter and tighter.

"You didn't answer my question. Are there others like you?"

The bird stopped and turned to face me. His beady eyes had taken on a solemn shade of midnight. "I wasn't always the greatest hunter on the island, you know. I was but one member of a cast of falcons. We were all the best at hunting, unstoppable together. But, one day, we were hunted instead."

"You got hunted? By whom?"

The bird began a dance of anxiety, switching between talons as he hopped. "The others, the born hunters. The Were-beasts. Oh, they're so terrible. They came and they took all of them away. Every last one! My whole world just vanished overnight!"

"I'm sorry," I said. Though he was technically still my captor, I felt a kinship to the lonely hunter. My world had also been taken away from me. "And now, you're the only one left?"

He nodded and crouched, rubbing his head on the ground.

"What are they like, the Were-beasts?"

"I don't want to talk about it," he said. "They're horrible abominations who only live to hunt innocent souls. Every ounce of pleasure in their lives comes at the cost of someone else's happiness. They came in while we lay sleeping, the cowards. You see, they only hunt at night, hidden in Mist."

"Ah, Do you mean mist like that mist over there?"

A sepia glaze was creeping into the orchard, leaking in through pores in the perimeter shrubbery. A thick vapor, it seemed to stick to all the space it filled. Even the moonlight was swallowed by its mass.

The bird was agitated. His dancing picked up in tempo. "This is bad. Oh, this is the worst thing that could happen! We won't get out of here alive. They're coming for me! They want to finish off the falcon cast, forever!"

"So, how about letting me down for now?" I begged. I didn't want to know what would happen when the mist reached me. I didn't want to see the Were-beasts. I didn't want to think of what they might do to Vespa if they caught her. What they might have already done. "Can you turn me into a trophy later? I promise I won't run away until then."

"Fine, fine," the bird squawked. "That's fine by me, except I don't know how to set you free."

"What do you mean?"

"I've never caught anything before. I don't know how to get you down!"

"Oh, please. Can't you just untie the knot?"

"No, that's falcon rope tied with a falcon knot. There's no way to untie it," the bird replied, puffing his chest full of pride.

"Well, could you hand me that blade down there? I can't quite reach it."

The falcon stared at my fallen machete for half a second, then scooped the knife into his maw and jumped onto my face. His fat talons pushed into my chin as he leaped higher, clawing his way up my jacket. With a haphazard jump he spun in the air, gripping the blade in his beak. The falcon's helicopter acrobatics sliced the rope above my ankle and dropped me onto my head in the dirt.

"Thanks, bird," I said, spitting dust away. "That was quite impressive. I didn't expect you could do something like that."

"Call me Downy," he said, clutching my blade beneath his wing. "When my cast wasn't hunting, we were performing. I might not look it, but I was the cast's resident acrobat. Now, get up, Trophy, we need to scram."

"I'm Charlie, by the way." It felt incredible to say that. "Nice to meet you, I guess."

The bird's beady eyes narrowed at me. "That's odd. You don't seem like much of a Charlie, to me. More like a Trophy."

I shrugged. "You don't seem like much of a hunter, but I can learn to deal with that. Can I have my knife back now?"

"Ha! You think I'm some sort of fool?" Downy ruffled his feathers. "You aren't a hunter, you don't know anything about this place. Don't forget, you're still my prize Trophy. I won't let anything happen to you, so I'll just hold onto this weapon for a bit. Let's move it, already."

My head nodded agreement, but my heart told me I couldn't leave. I fruitlessly scanned the orchard one last time for Vespa. As I was about to yield to the angry falcon pulling on my pant legs, Hammond's bowl caught my eye. I couldn't bear to leave it behind.

Tearing free from my captor, I dashed with all my speed to grab the shallow wooden dish. Reaching for it, I slipped and fell, staining my purple jeans with grass juice. I clambered to my knees and grabbed for the bowl, dodging a wayward tendril of mist.

The heavy mist let out a soft hiss as it slipped by my ear. I rolled away, bowl clutched to my chest, as more vaporous tentacles grasped for the spots my body had just vacated. My primal senses told me that a single touch from the gaseous amoeba would mean my imminent demise. Death's fingers at my rear, a sublime force drove me away to safety. I dared not stop to look back. My feet somehow worked themselves below my body and I found myself running at full tilt back to Downy's tree. He had retrieved his rope and fashioned himself a makeshift sword belt.

"Hey!" he shouted, "Don't go risking my trophy like that, Trophy. It's not fair! Are you going to come with me this time? Do you want to live to see the sunrise?"

I nodded, shivering. Though I had escaped the mist's touch, its dreadful aura had charred my spirit. Terror lurked inside the mists. I hoped I would never know its true shape.

While my friendly foe forged forward into the foliage, I gave in to curiosity and turned for one last glimpse at the orchard. Just an hour ago, the grove had been a prismatic mosaic, the epitome of visual diversity. The mist had transformed the spectacle into a monochromatic wasteland. That garden would be a place forever etched into my mind, a hallowed ground where my new identity had been born. I couldn't bear to forget it.

"Vespa," I whispered, watching the mists devour the remaining bits of orchard. "I hope you knew where you were going."

SWELL

Downy and I moved in silence, but the travel was slow. This branch of the forest was devoid of any path or luxury. The falcon led me with an invisible leash, the bond of mutual survival. He slipped through the underbrush to forge a path forward. I followed him with nothing but blind faith, hoping his hunter's instincts would lead us to safety. At the very least, we moved away from the mists.

I lost track of the time we spent pushing on and on. Shadows tricked my eyes, as I grew more tired. I swore that tiny shadow monsters dashed alongside us, keeping pace, just waiting for us to falter. But, none showed their faces. A flawless, full moon shone bright above us, gilding the foliage in dim, ambient light.

Downy came to a sudden stop and turned to address me. "We've got to change direction, this path is no good for us."

"Why's that?"

"This wall right here? We can't get through."

I caught up to the falcon and touched the rock face. From a distance, it looked solid black; up close I could see it was a subterranean azure, faintly transparent. It was tall, smooth, and slick as a whistle. In any other circumstances, it would have been breathtaking. "What is this?" I asked.

"The Ring? It's the thing keeping us from where we want to be going! Don't you know anything?"

"But, how did it get here? It's so big! Is it natural?"

"Yes, it's nature's beautiful obstacle, stopping us from achieving happiness. And, by happiness, I mean survival. Now, we just need to get on the other side. If only I could tell exactly where we are standing, I could take us to a path that slips right through."

"There's no way we can scale it, is there? It's much too slippery. Gosh, I wonder what it's made of?"

"Will you focus, please? Remember, we're on the run from horrible Were-beasts. This wall is forcing us to change our direction." Downy turned to face me and spread his wings to either side. "Pick a wing, trophy."

"Why am I deciding? Aren't you a little more familiar with this territory, Downy? Don't you hunt these grounds and live here?"

"Well, I don't have very good night vision. So, I really don't know where we are, right now. I don't know which way is up or down, out here. See, I live on the inside of the Ring and don't have reason to spend much time outside."

"Why were you hunting outside the Ring today?"

"Oh, just woke up with a hunch that I'd catch a pretty little thing if I cast a net or two out here. To be honest, I've never been hunting on this side of the Ring."

I gave him my best stink eye, but it was lost in the darkness. "Are you sure you're a hunter? I think you're mostly crazy."

"Right, sure!" he said, ire bubbling through his voice. "Right as rain falls downwards. Now, come on! Right or left wing?"

I closed my eyes and tried to imagine what Vespa would do if she were here. I visualized her approaching the wall and stroking it with her delicate fingers. I watched as her simulacrum pressed her ears to the cool, flat surface and listened to the Ring's ancient language. Then Vespa turned and brushed her lips on the wall as thanks. She kissed it twice or thrice or a dozen times more before my dream was scattered into ten million shards by a thrashing falcon.

"Hurry it up already! I can smell the Mists coming this way. We've got to move now unless you want to get hunted again tonight."

"All right," I assured him. "Let's go to the right. Hopefully, we'll find a way through before that nasty fog catches up to us."

Our progress was swift along the cliff face. There was a ghost of a path sidled up against the natural barrier; no plants grew within several feet of the wall, not even grass. All the tree trunks tilted away from the Ring, as if running in terror. Their seeds fell further from the towering bluffs with every generation, a slow but steady retreat.

With each step forward, an ophidian hiss grew louder. It came from nothing, but was everywhere. The pores of the earth were raging! I swallowed lumps of terror, but Downy pressed on and I grabbed hold of his courage. After a few minutes travel, we reached a terrible juxtaposition of opportunity and fate.

A great, forty meter crevasse split the cliff into two massive walls, allowing us passage into the center of the Ring. However, a rushing river filled the gap from wall to wall. It was an artery pumping rich blood to thirsty veins and capillaries deeper in the island. The river lay too wide and its water flowed too fast for us to forge across it.

"Even if we could cross, I wouldn't recommend it," Downy offered. "Look carefully across the way."

I squinted through the dark river spray across the river. My hope eroded.

"The mist has covered every inch of that shore," I said, "Even if we made it over before getting sucked away by the current, the mist would envelop us on the beach. We're screwed! But, why is it just sitting there? Won't it try to come across and reach us?"

"Have you ever heard of a Mist that crosses moving water?" asked Downy. "No, neither have I."

"But, aren't mists just made of water's vapors? Wouldn't they love to float above the surface of the river? In fact, wouldn't that make them grow stronger?"

"I don't know what weird mist you're talking about, Trophy, but I think I know a thing or two about Mist. We've got no time to spare. If we wait long enough, that creeping vapor will sneak around behind us and cover every inch of this shore, too. You won't like that very much."

"Well, okay." I said. "I guess there's no other option." I looked down the river's flow, through the crevasse. It disappeared beyond a sharp turn after a short distance. What river I could see was trapped on either side by steep, tall cliffs. "How do we do this? Should we just jump in? Can you swim?"

"That is none of your business," Downy stated, ruffling his crest. "And it doesn't matter, we'll just take my boat."

"Your what?"

"My boat, Trophy. Since you are my trophy, so is that boat you risked your life to recover. I order you to use it so we may travel down the river in lavish style and comfort."

Still confused, I looked at the only thing he could have been mentioning. "My bowl? You want to ride in my bowl? No way. I don't think this thing even floats."

"I don't care what you want to call that thing," Downy chimed, "But, I know a boat when I see one. That, Trophy, is a boat. So, put it in the water, get us aboard, and let's go already!"

My eyes reflexively rolled up in their sockets. "Fine. I'll give it a shot."

I placed the bowl in the shallows and we both climbed in. There was plenty of room for me to sit comfortably, with Downy perched on the edge opposite me. Our weights balanced the dish enough to keep it afloat without tipping it over. The bowl's floating ability was unbelievable. The travel was so smooth I was sure the wood wasn't even touching the water. The bowl's curved belly glided right on top of the current like a hovercraft. With a kick off of the shore, we began spinning down the river. We drifted downstream between the majestic, obsidian walls on either side of the valley.

The mouth of the cliff pass shrank merrily as we ambled on our way. As our voyage entered its first sharp turn, just before the banks swept out of view, a heavy coat of Mist rolled onto the shore. It spilled over into the river, but fizzed into nothingness at the water's touch. Vaporous tendrils molested the air, groping at null and void.

The Mist appeared angry, writhing in rage. It had spent all night searching for Downy and me and was throwing a fit of frustration at our escape. I knew this imagery to be quite silly, but couldn't help myself. I half expected the Mist to be shaking a Mist fist in the air, cursing my very existence. I had to laugh after our narrow escape. As I chuckled to myself, relief flooded my bones. Our safety was assured at last. The Mist could not follow us down this sacred channel.

I drew my attention back to my immediate surroundings. Downy clutched the edge of the bowl for dear life, peering deep into our vessel's wake. The walls of this part of the channel glowed pale blue, an inner light awakening as night fell.

The light was intense enough to illuminate the rhythmic waves. I looked into the sparkling water and able to see myself for the first time. My face appeared pale and soft. I was disappointed; my features were set a bit wider than I expected. My nose looked like a blob of mud that someone had seen fit to attach to the center of my face. My reflection and I squeezed our nose. It didn't feel as soft as it looked. My hair was brown and loud, poofing out in all directions. Everything about my appearance was so different from Vespa and her delicate features. She might as well have been born of a different species.

For half a second, I saw her reflection on the wave next to mine, winking at me with those unstoppable eyes. When the water settled again, I saw it was a different pale shape keeping me company. I looked upwards, my vision narrowed by the blinding bluffs. The sky was blank but for its signature white orb. The massive pearl was responsible for the glowing cliffs, the shining shore, and my terrible longing.

I hoped Vespa was looking at the same moon and empty sky, somewhere on the island. They would probably be invisible from inside the Mists.

"Hey, Downy, I've been meaning to ask you something. Did you see a girl with bright pink hair leave the orchard last night?"

The bird tilted his beak and ruffled his feathers, still staring at the bowl's wake. "No, I never saw a girl last night, definitely not one with pink hair. She must be much more apt at survival than you. Why do you ask?"

"Well, there was a girl with me last night. But, she disappeared shortly before you caught me. We were talking about some stuff, I think I upset her, and she just took off. I'm worried that she didn't think to escape the Mist's grasp. She's new to the island, like me."

Downy emitted some excited chirps and bobbed his head. "There's another girl like you wandering about, lost and alone? Well, we've got to go track her down. I don't like the thought of one of the Were-beasts catching her. They'll do terrible, terrible things to people like you. Oh, yes, they hate everything without wings even more than they hate everything with wings."

"Thanks, I'm glad you agree. Can we go look for her as soon as we find a place to dock and step ashore?"

"Yes, that's a great idea, Trophy. Oh, I'm so excited. Don't worry. We'll get this girl back in one piece. I promise!"

"Excellent, Downy! I'm glad we agree. You know, I'm glad we're starting to get along a little better. You really aren't such a bad bird. Maybe we can start to be friends."

"Oh, I'm quite the good bird. A good hunter, too. With a pair of gems like you two, I can make a set of matching trophies unlike anything this island has ever seen! I promise not to stuff you in lewd positions or anything disrespectful. No, I like you too much for that. You're rather charming, for something so easily captured."

"Hey!" I shouted. "Don't even joke about that!" I reached over to swat the bird, upsetting our delicate balance. The ship rocked, spinning faster than before.

"Stop that!" Downy squawked. "Stop whatever that was! You're upsetting me! You're upsetting the boat! Can't you see I'm busy?"

"Yeah, you're looking pretty intensely at the water. What do you see down there? Some tasty morsel? Your beautiful face?"

Downy hissed at me. "I'm not kidding now," he whispered. "You've got to be quiet. I think we're being followed. Something else was running from the Mists, and it's stalking us. Shut your mouth and help me watch for it. Your eyes are probably better than mine at night."

Thoroughly whipped, I reseated my ass in silence. The bowl was spinning at a fair rate, so Downy and I watched the waters over each other's shoulders. A stifling silence fell between us, so strong it muffled my rambling brain.

I saw our pursuer first. A woman's head was bobbing many meters upstream of our vessel. She appeared to be treading water, but was struggling to stay afloat. Her pale hands and face caught the light of the moon and glistened. Gossamer threads shined pink on the top of her head.

My voice leapt out my throat before my heart or brain could filter anything. "Vespa! Vespa, come here! Get on our boat, there's something in the water!"

"What are you doing?" Downy hissed. "Can't you see what that is? You just sank us, you rotten gold rumbly!"

It was too late to escape. The woman paddled towards the bowl, growing faster by the second, multiplying the current by the speed of her strokes.

I ignored my companion's manic mumbling. "Vespa, you're almost here! Just a little bit further and you can reach my hands."

I rotated myself, careful not to rock the boat, and extended my arm to greet the sweet girl who had followed us down the river. She reached her hand out of the water a splash length away from mine. As our fingers closed, about to brush tips, I felt electricity in the air. This excitement was grounded, when Downy pulled me away by the seat of my pants.

As I fell back into the bowl, the unmistakable sound of snapping jaws filled the air. In the place where my hand had dangled, a set of shiny, jagged teeth snapped shut. Slender stems attached Vespa's head and arms to a gnashing, gnarly maw. The dire jaws jutted out from on the front end of a long, serpentine body undulating just beneath the waves.

"It's a Were-fish!" Downy yelled. "No escape! We've got to separate to survive! You would have made a fine trophy, Trophy. Goodbye!"

Without another word, Downy dove off the front end of the dish and flopped downstream as fast as his flapping wings would pull him.

I knew the bird was right, though he was a terrible coward. Sitting in the bowl would do me no good. The Were-fish swam out a few dozen feet behind the bowl, preparing to strike again. This was his turf; I had to play by his rules.

I dove off the bowl, perpendicular to the path of the river. As I kicked the bowl away, I felt the Were-beast's powerful jaws snap shut, inches from my feet. The fish propelled itself forward, its long body making a tremendous splash upon reentering the water. Its momentum carried it forward, beyond my position. I watched as the serpentine body slithered past me, just under the surface of the water. Tiny bat-wings along the beast's spine acted as flippers, spurring it faster down the stream. I half-hoped it was chasing after Downy, the little yellow bastard. He had a little head start, at least.

My water-treading instincts took over as I attempted to hold my ground. The current was too strong for me to swim upstream; the Were-beast's maw awaited me down around the next bend.

Treading water and drifting downstream was my best bet for survival. At least, I knew I wouldn't drown.

I waited as my body meandered down the liquid path. The sky was beginning to lighten again. I recognized the familiar, feverous blend of morning colors. The morning felt like another rebirth, though this time I had a name and a few memories to call my own. I was enamored by the sky's beauty when a pair of spindly hands grabbed my dangling ankles and dragged me underneath the current.

CREST

The Were-fish locked its hands around my ankles. Tiny spines on its palms spewed venom into my blood. My racing heart pumped the toxins through every last vein in my body. The venom's malicious effect siphoned away my will to escape. I let the beast pull me where it would.

As the fish dragged my body deeper into the river's belly, I couldn't help but think my predicament an ironic way to die. I was born on the shore, evicted by the sea for some unknown reason. I would drown beneath the surface of different waters, still lacking understanding. For some reason, my imminent death didn't bother me too much. It wasn't as though I was losing much. The time I had spent awake on the island was all I could be sure had composed my life. My time awake had been shorter than a mayfly's entire life cycle. More troubling to me was the inanity of it all. I had never found a purpose or a reason to be. Even worse, I would never understand exactly what made Vespa so magical.

I blinked and saw endless blue. The surface, walls, and floor of the river melted together, indistinguishable to my eyes as the beast dragged me ever deeper. The Were-fish swam so fast I couldn't tell whether we were moving upstream or down or if we had stopped altogether. The only sound at this depth was my sibilant captor, zooming on and on. My awareness caved to the aggregate pressures of depth and fear, pushing my waking thoughts into a realm of dreams.

The cerulean substance permeating my vision faded to sepia and lost its moist density. I stood in the midst of thick Mist, trapped in the prison I had tried so hard to avoid. I tried to move forward, but my feet did not comply with their instructions. They ignored me to the point that I wondered if they were still attached to the ends of my legs. The fog below my waist was so thick I couldn't check on my pedals.

As far as I could tell, there was no ground, no sky, no end to the vapors of this realm. I floated in a bizarre world of intangible thoughts, passing in and out of existence faster than they could be caught and examined. Everywhere I turned my head, swirling ripples of Mist painted half-pictures and whispered half-truths directly to my brain.

You must cease to be. You are not welcome in this realm, they told me.

"Believe me, I don't want to be here," I replied. "I'm here by accident, I assure you! I will just be going now."

It is unsafe for you to remain here. You endanger more than you realize. More than you have the right to threaten.

"Then tell me how to get out of here. I'm more than willing to leave. I don't want to hurt anybody."

It is not that simple, Wingless boy. You are trapped in this realm and cannot escape by your will alone. Only on the back of another will you return o your original state safe and intact.

"But I came in alone. Can't I escape alone?"

You cannot escape; you may only return to whence you came.

"And where is that? Am I going to die now? Is this the afterlife? What do you want of me? Let me be free!"

I waited but the voice gave me no answers. The Mists hypnotized me further with scenes of abstract angels and tangrammed devils flirting amidst monochromatic, coiling tendrils. The tiny deities flitted about leaving streams of nonexistence in their wakes. I watched aeronaut-spiders streak over limpid whorls before exploding in a muffled puff. Dragon's breath raged through incorporeal cities, razing them to the invisible ground. A voluptuous wisp beckoned me toward an eccentric spiral. Beyond them all, a great, hooded figure loomed. It extended its arms, palms down, as though it were leading some unseen puppets in a synchronized dance. The figure turned its darkened face toward me and bellowed.

Whatever shackles chained my feet released without warning. I flew forward out of control. My body spun counter to the wisp's spiral. She giggled and clapped, enjoying my terrified grunts. I collided with her ethereal vortex and we fused together in an unsavory whole. Like an ethereal meat-grinder, the spiral sliced through my being and warped my senses to the point of breaking. Every part of my conscious self stretched and stretched until it snapped.

I opened my mouth to scream, but Mist flooded in like I'd switched on a vacuum. Not a mote of sound escaped. I was helpless, trapped under a heavy beige blanket for what felt like a century. I lay paralyzed until the world shimmered into black.

The first sight to greet my waterlogged eyes was the Were-fish's dangling lure, bobbing inches from my face. I jolted upright and flailed my limbs like a primeval man.

"Hey there, Charlie," the lure said, "How've you been? It's nice to see you again!"

As my nerves flickered back to normal levels, I took in my surroundings. I was sitting in an oversized bed, located in a well lit, dry location. The monster at my bedside was none other than Vespa, safe from the terrors of the night. I leapt forward and squeezed her with a mighty hug.

"You made it!" I cried. "I was so worried you'd been nabbed by the Mists."

"Really?" she asked, nudging me back into the bed. "You were worried about me? That's adorable. I was fine. I didn't have any trouble at all. Didn't see any Mists, that's for sure! Really, you should be happier that you're safe. After all, if they hadn't shown up when they did, you'd be Were-fish food by now."

"Who are they?" I asked, realizing we were not alone.

Behind Vespa, near the door to my suite, loomed two of the biggest birds I had ever seen. These birds dwarfed Hammond by a good three feet and made him look emaciated. Their big white bellies jutted out between flat, webbed feet and elegant heads. Flaming yellow and red feathers dangled from their temples down past their orange beaks. Their backs, sides, and human-sized flippers shined a sleek black, like the bottom of a capsized kayak.

"Hullo there," the bird on the left spoke, its tone deep and rubbery. "I'm glad to see you up and well."

"Thanks," I replied, "Who are you, again?"

"Oh, forgive him," said the other bird. "My name is Beverly, this is my partner Quinn. This is one of our humble apartments. I know it's not much, but please make yourself at home as long as you are staying here."

I guessed Beverly was a female from the sound of her voice, like submerged bells. However, I couldn't find any visual clues to distinguish her from Quinn. "Well, thank you for that. It sounds like I owe you a great deal of gratitude."

Quinn flapped his flipper flippantly. "Oh, no worries. We were just out fishing when we bumped into that nasty fish. He looked like he was going to eat you, and you didn't look too happy about it. So, we rescued you. It was two birds with one spear! No biggie."

"Even so, I'm extremely grateful that you found me when you did. I was sure I wouldn't survive that encounter."

"It was a particularly nasty fish, that one," Quinn stated, "Much more violent than any we've run across before. It almost put up a fight before we pierced it."

"Yes," Beverly agreed. "It was quite unexpected, but a fortuitous find. That one fish alone will feed the whole colony for a night!"

I rubbed my eyes for a moment. "I'm sorry. The colony?"

Beverly nodded her massive head, shaking her entire body in the process. "Welcome to Helmsdotter, the drifters colony. Our family, a colony of albatrosses, founded it ages ago, but anybody is welcome to rest here. However, little rest turns into quite the long stay! When creatures get lost on the Island, they are usually either eaten by the Were-beasts or they end up here."

"The Were-beasts? Do they really kill that many people?" I asked, despite already knowing the answer. My thoughts turned to Downy, my missing companion. There was no trace of that falcon in the apartment.

The albatross couple glanced at each other. Each bird's eyes urged the other to speak.

"Well, I'm not sure exactly what to tell you. The Were-beasts are somewhat taboo in the colony," Beverly mentioned. "Most folks here have lost family or friends to them. Otherwise, they probably would not have come to seek sanctuary."

Quinn finished his partner's thoughts. "I don't think you should mention the Weres around the colony, especially in these happy days. There's no reason to dampen spirits. Today is a joyous day for frabjous fun!"

"What's so special about today?" I asked, rubbing my eyes. The Were-fish's venom had left me feeling like I would never want to party again.

Vespa nudged me and winked. "We arrived just in time to celebrate Palm Sunday! Aren't you excited?"

"I don't know. Should I be? What's the deal?"

"Palm Sunday!" Quinn said, "It's the best day of the year. It's my favorite time to play and jive, the very best time to be alive!"

"It's the day that Helmsdotter was founded," Beverly clarified. "One hundred years ago, our grandalbatrosses came together at this spot and decided to make a haven for lost souls. On that very day, the palm lilies all over the lake bloomed at once. Every year since then, Palm Sunday marks the day that the palm lilies open their hearts and release their euphoric aroma for us to enjoy."

"And there are fireworks and feasts and dancing!" Quinn continued. "That fish we caught is going to be the main course this year, with rumbly sauce. Oh, it's such an honor to provide a Palm Sunday fish!"

Quinn's excitement was contagious; I was infected at once. The antidote for Were-fish venom was, apparently, albatross smiles. "Ha! I guess I should be honored too, right? After all, if it hadn't been chasing after me then you never would have seen it in the first place."

The albatrosses nearly fell over laughing. Fortunately, they remained upright. I'm not sure how birds of their girth could right themselves, once toppled. I would have been crushed in any attempt to help. Vespa stood aloof, but her arms crossed beneath her chest and an unfathomable smirk trickled across her mouth. Was she thinking the same thing as me? I wondered if the night would end up being a good night to party after all.

"I'm sorry," Beverly said, nudging Quinn. "It looks like you two might need to catch up on a few things. We'll leave you be for now. Remember, Vespa, The Seer asked that you attend an audience with her, when you are able. She wants to speak to you both before tonight's festivities. It's important!"

We thanked them for their hospitality and they waddled out of the room, leaving Vespa and me alone. Leaving us in silence that I couldn't wait to break.

"Vespa, how did you make it here? Last time we met, you left so quickly, before we could really make any plans. But, I was really worried about you."

"I'm sorry about that," she said, "I needed to be alone for a bit and travel through my thoughts. I just took off in one direction and didn't look back. I traveled along those dark cliffs until I found a path to take me through. It was a long, dark tunnel. I couldn't see even a few feet in front of my face it was so completely black. I just kept walking all night until I saw some moonlight at the other end. When I finally reached the end of the tunnel, it put me out right on the shore of this lake. I saw the shining pyramid floating in the middle of the lake, so I swam out to it, hoping to run into somebody. Anybody, really. I'm not going to lie, it was a bit scary outside the orchard."

"You're telling me! The Mist almost caught us! It was right behind us, breathing its moist breath down our necks. Wait, we're in the middle of a lake? On a shiny pyramid?"

"Yep, Helmsdotter is a big, glittering pyramid. Apparently, the pyramid is built in the center of a lake, which is the center of this island. The island is a giant ring around this place, because it's a big, flooded crater. We could be sitting in the center of a giant, dormant volcano! And, I hear it's not completely dead. It could revive itself any day! Isn't that cool?"

"Really? Well, that's not exactly the most settling news. No, I'm not entirely okay with that. In fact, not at all. Why did the albatrosses have to build a colony on the most dangerous part of the island?"

"Well, if you had to live in a volcano, wouldn't you like to live in a place surrounded by water? Extra protection!"

A flicker of our previous conversation flashed through my head. "Wait a second, you swam out to the pyramid? I thought you said you didn't know how to swim?"

"No, that's silly," Vespa said, "You must have misheard me."

"I'm quite certain. You said that the reason we couldn't escape the island on a raft was because you couldn't swim and would probably die. That it wasn't worth the risk!"

"I'm sorry, Charlie, but you must be mistaken. Obviously, I can swim. I wouldn't be here if I couldn't. I don't know what I said to you, but I wouldn't outright lie. I'm much sweeter than that, I promise!"

"Fine," I said, too-exhausted to argue. "It seems that you can swim. You still haven't explained why you left in such a hurry."

"I'm sorry!" she exclaimed, voice tense. "I didn't realize you'd be such a turd about it. I just got upset and had to leave. I wasn't in the mood to explain myself to you, and now I've even forgotten why I got so mad. Let's just chalk it up to craziness or hormones and leave it alone. Will that satisfy you? Can we move on to something else now?"

As if in response, my stomach churned out a heavy growl. "Well, I am starving! I haven't eaten a thing since those rumblies. Can we get some food around here?"

Vespa clapped her hands once, emitting a short energy burst that shattered the descending awkwardness. "Already so many steps ahead of

63

you! Quinn and Beverly brought us some cheeses and bread. They filled up that bowl of yours to the brim!"

I followed Vespa's extended arm to the table beside my bed. My bowl was sitting comfortable and dry with nary a scratch, filled with a variety of loaves and hunks. Just looking at the pile filled my nose with a musty rainbow of fungal odor. It smelled divine.

"That is Hammond's bowl! I didn't expect to see it again. Wherever did they find it?"

Vespa shrugged. "They brought it back with you when they captured that tasty looking Were-fish. But, is that what you ought to be worried about right now?"

I shook my head like a baby's rattle and grabbed an especially moldy looking hunk and bit into it. Musty fragrance exploded onto my pallet. The savory stench served to whet my appetite even further. I pulled the bowl onto the bed and gestured that Vespa should sit and join me. We sat in silence and stuffed our faces. Vespa's familiar grin slipped over her lips again as I choked on a hunk of puckeringly sour dough.

After hacking and wheezing for a minute, I was able to breathe and speak once more. "So, they just found me and the bowl? You didn't notice any other birds showing up around the same time as I did?"

"No," Vespa shook her head, "Not that I know of. Why? Were you expecting someone?"

"Well," I started, "After you left, I guess I made a friend. I'm not sure that's the right word for him, exactly, but I liked him well enough to wonder if he's all right."

Vespa crammed the heel of a pumpernickel loaf into her mouth. "Nopf, 'aven't 'eard noffing. Forry about that." Dark crumbs dribbled down her pink blouse. It was colored by wavelength of light that matched her hair to the nanometer.

"That's very attractive," I teased.

In defense, Vespa poked me with the rest of her pumpernickel baguette. I picked up a flaxseed batard to fend off her attacks, parrying with all my ability. We jumped to our feet, trading blows for several minutes. Vespa slipped by my seedy defense and jabbed my ribcage.

"Ha! Now, you're cursed by the devil's fart!" she jested. "That'll teach you. Just do whatever I want and agree with everything I say or you'll get a heel to the gut, got it?"

"Yes'm. As of this moment, I cede all our future battles. I give you my word!"

Vespa laughed and swallowed the rest of her sword. "We should get going now. I don't want to be late for tonight's ceremonies! I had Quinn show me the way to the seer's quarters while you slept. Don't worry, it's a quick walk."

"Okay, but I have a quick question. How long was I out?"

"Oh, maybe three or four days? You conked out!"

"I've been asleep for days! No wonder I was hungry. I didn't think that was even possible!"

"Mmmhmmm, hurry up and finish!"

I scarfed down the rest of my stinky cheese and Vespa dragged me out of the comfortable bedroom.

She pulled me down an albatross-sized corridor. Rough, stone walls converged at the top, negating the need for a true ceiling. Human-sized torches stuck out from the walls next to large wooden doors. All the doors were built from solid slabs of wood, nary a mark to distinguish one from another. We passed by many adjoining halls that looked identical to the path we traveled. Vespa turned us right, then left, then right, right, left, and right and I swore we hadn't moved an inch.

"Are you sure you..." I began.

She cut me off with a hiss. "Shh! I know where I'm going. Mostly. Well, I know what I'm looking for, at the very least."

"Well, I already doubt if I could find my way back to the apartment. I don't know how you're-"

"Here we are!" Vespa said, braking hard. "This is it, the seer's apartment."

There was no question; we had found the right place. While the other doors we had seen stood plain and tall, this door was an extravagant masterwork. The Seer's door was adorned with a vast array of gaudy symbols and icons. Six unnamed albatrosses swam around what was either the moon or a big wheel of cheese. Sparkling stars covered the rest of the door, coated by thick layers of glitter. The stars formed unfamiliar constellations, through which swam all manners of strange beasts. In the lower right corner, I noticed a tiny Were-fish staring back at me. The little Vespa-head on its lure stirred fearful memories in the pit of my stomach.

"We should go in now, yes?" I asked, eager to escape the Were-fish's malevolent eye.

Despite the door being twice her size, Vespa easily pushed it in and stepped into the dark beyond. As she disappeared inside, a thin tendril of smoke poured out from the threshold, beckoning me to follow. My mind flashed to the grasping Mist I had narrowly escaped so recently. Gulping my terror away, I plunged into the seer's quarters, succumbing to the darkness and smoke.

BREAK

A thin veil of smoke tinted everything in the seer's apartment with a green-grey sheen, like moist avocados. The room smelled of freshly plucked mandrake. Pungent yet enticing, the scent caused a train wreck in my nose. Vespa was waving at me from the middle of the quarter, sitting with who I guessed was the seer.

She was an albatross like the others, but she carried an air of prestige about her. Instead of a boat's hull, her skin resembled used sandpaper. The seer's beak was widened by age, more resembling a mask than an eating utensil. Her eye-feathers drooped like golden anacondas slithering down the sides of her body. That ancient body lounged on a green, velvet couch as the seer pulled smoke from a hookah set before her. I wondered if the couch had originally been green, or if years of smoke had tinted it beyond recognition.

"Come here, Charlie," Vespa beckoned in her dulcet tone. "Sit down with me. The seer has been waiting for us all day! Let's not delay her any more."

"Thank you for coming to join me," the seer rasped, her voice thick with an accent acquired by years of smoking. "I'm glad to meet you both. There aren't many Wingless that make their way to Helmsdotter. And humans, no less! It is an honor for our paths to cross."

I bowed and jumped into a chair next to Vespa. "It's an honor to be here," we said, at once.

Vespa raised her brow and mouthed a silent jinx my way. I felt nothing, but prayed that her magic would be dampened by the seer's mystic presence. I didn't want to embarrass myself any more than necessary, and her spells could make such a fool of me.

"I trust my grandchildren have treated you well?"

Vespa nodded and I shrugged. I hadn't realized the seer was related to my saviors.

"They mean well, they want to help, but they were not blessed with the gifts of my blood. I am the last seer of the colony," the seer emphasized. "My astral powers, too, are limited. Oh, how they wane with age. Still, they are stronger than those of the average beast or bird.

"I know not what you seek; I know not why you are here. However, I wish to use my powers to help you find where you are meant to be. I will pray that you may find your true destiny, aided by my wings and my wisdom." She paused to take a puff of the hookah, releasing it through her nostrils. The curls of smoke made her appear threatening, like a sleepy dragon.

"We are grateful for your aid, most powerful seer," Vespa said. "It is an unnecessary gift, but a most welcome one!" I nodded agreement.

"Don't bother with all that formality," the seer said. "Just call me Seer."

Seer took a strong pull from the hookah and blew a series of smoke six rings. She puffed a smoke albatross that flew up through the middle of the rings, bursting the line one-by-one.

"Please, inform my cloudy mind. How did you each come to the Island?"

"I just woke up on the shore," I said, "Pure as the day I was conceived. I had no memories or identity. I've made some new memories since waking, but I still have no idea about my old self. Can you tell me where I came from?"

"I came in from the sky," Vespa said, "I was out skydiving with my family, but I unleashed my parachute too soon. A super strong wind picked me up and plucked me away from my group. It carried me all the way here. Can you tell me if my parents are here on the island?"

"Wait a second," I interrupted, "That's not the story you told me! You said that your plane was malfunctioning; you got ripped out of your seat when the door opened and fell to the ground!" I worried for a second, about Vespa's memory. Had something happened to her in the night? Had the Mist laid a tendril on her mind?

Vespa wrinkled her nose at me. "I don't think so. I mean, maybe I said something like that, but what I meant was that I was skydiving. I think you need to work on your listening abilities, Charlie."

I opened my mouth to snip out a reply, but Seer spoke before I could eke out a sound. Her deep vibrations reversed the tension's momentum.

"This island has that effect on people," she said, "The things we hold most dear have a naughty way of slipping from us. I have known many flocks of birds that stop in to rest during a migration, never to resume their journey. They forget where they were headed to begin with. Worse yet, some even forget that they can fly. The most valiant knight can lose his purpose. The Island's atmosphere will strip him of his quest."

Seer paused to take a drag of hashish, but Vespa and I remained silent. We both sat rapt, eager to consume her next words. Having sated her lungs, the Seer exhaled her next question with a billow of smoke.

"What is it that you seek most desperately?"

"I want to get off this island," Vespa said, "And, I want to go home. I want to get back to my other comfortable life. I want to find my parents. And, I want fresh underpants."

"I agree," I started, "At least, I think I do. I mean, I don't know if I need clean underpants. And I still don't know if my home is a place I want to find. Maybe I ran away from a bad situation? What can you tell me of my past?"

Seer pondered our answers as she smoked. "It seems," she said, after some time, "That neither of you really knows what you want. And, as such, I cannot help you. If you spend some more time on the Island, you may find your wishes will come true before you even know what they are meant to be."

"Stop!" Vespa yelled. "I am quite certain of what I want. I want to get home! I don't want to be stranded here forever! I was someone, once! Someone important!"

"You don't know what kind of life you are wishing for," Seer said. "It's slipping from you, girl. Soon enough, you'll know as little about your old home as Charlie knows about his. Maybe you've already forgotten it."

This quieted, but did not satisfy Vespa. She crossed her arms and stared down the most powerful bird in Helmsdotter. The heat of her eyes told me she was thinking of the many ways that albatross might be prepared to eat.

Seer was unfazed by the hostility, if she noticed it at all. "I have a feeling that you have more questions yet unanswered. I invited you here so that I might put your hearts at ease, at least for a while. Please, feel free to ask anything."

"Does the island have a name?" I blurted, tired of referring to the landmass as an oblique entity.

"You cannot name that which is in constant flux. Some people try to name the Island, but they soon find their choice improper and invalid. Naming a thing gives it power, but also lashes a chain of specificity around it. This island will be bound by nothing. So, it remains the Island, now and forever."

"So, there isn't a proper name for it?"

"No. Like the Island, I gave up my proper name long ago. I recommend you try it sometime. I think you'll find it can be quite liberating. Keep in mind, I am still Seer rather than a seer, just as the Island is not the island. Do you understand?"

"No," I blustered, "No, I do not. I rather like having a name, thank you very much. Before I had a name, I didn't know anything about myself. From my name, I've built up something like a self. Living without an identity isn't really living at all."

The Seer nodded. "Yes, I can see how you might think that. Perhaps you are right, but I fear that your name will bring you misery before long. You, too, will grow tired of the chain lashing your self to this identity. Or, perhaps you will grow too attached. It's just something to keep in your mind's eye."

I felt a deep ire rising from my gut. Vespa had given me my name. The Seer had just launched a double-pronged insult to my pride and my friend.

"You ready to go, Charlie?" Vespa asked. "I've learned just about all I care to, for the day." Her eyes told me she had heard the insult, as well.

I nodded agreement and stood to leave. Seer clapped her flippers together with a wet smack of authority, shocking me back into my seat.

"You, boy," she beckoned, "Stay a moment. I would speak to you alone."

I nodded to Vespa as she took her leave. Surely, Seer bore me no more ill will. She couldn't upset me much more than she already had.

"Stay seated," she began, "I have urgent words of warning. I entreat you to heed them well, and keep them to yourself."

"I'm listening," I said. "But I'm not sure I want to hear whatever you have to say."

Seer ignored me and continued. "Bad omens rise with the coming of the Crow moon. The Were-beasts usually remain confined to the realm of Mists. Their presence in our lands is a sure sign that the order of the Island is shifting, realigning itself. Everything is changing. It is but a matter of time before the Island is overrun and we are all less than dead. Devoured. Erased!"

"Why are you telling this to me? I don't even know how I could be less than dead! If this is true, then it is vital that all the Helmsdotterians know! We can't just keep this between us."

"I told you, just listen! I'm telling you this because it is your fault these disasters are arising! Change of this magnitude doesn't just happen on the Island! Something has got to trigger it, a cascading effect. And the biggest thing different about the Island is you!" Seer shouted. I had little power against her normal tone, but her forte pinned me to my seat. "I'm doing this for your sake, human boy. If all my people knew this was your fault, do you think they would welcome you as they do? No, you would be cast into the waters for another wayward Were-fish to devour."

I was stunned. "I don't believe you! I haven't done anything to cause something like this to happen. How can you know this is true? And why are you accusing me? What about Vespa?"

"Ha! Don't blame the girl! That's so unlike you, Charlie. Or, is it? Maybe you're a selfish misogynist, after all. You heard the story of Palm Sunday, did you not?" Seer croaked. "You heard the story that most bird-folk tell of Helmsdotter's founding? Of the beautiful lilies blossoming on the same day every year?"

"Yes," I replied. "That's what I was told."

"Well, it's a half truth, you see," the old crone began. "This colony has been around much longer than that silly holiday.

"There was another boy like you, once. He came to our pyramid looking for answers, much like you do now. He did not understand that he brought with him an unsolvable dilemma, a puzzle that my people were not meant to unravel. Though he entered alone, the Were-beasts followed him into the pyramid mere days after his arrival. The Mist normally can't reach us here beyond our little moat. However, as you have seen, the beasts are quite capable of leaving their sanctuary. Though it left them vulnerable, they wanted to find this boy most at any cost. So, they showed up in our halls and devoured most of Helmsdotter's people as they searched for him. A few warriors resisted, of course, but by the end of it, all of them lay slaughtered. Only when the vagrant boy disappeared did our home return to peace.

"That day was the true inspiration behind Palm Sunday. When the Were-beasts vanished, when the waters ceased to run red with bird-blood, the survivors celebrated to excess unheard of on all the Islands of the multiverse. The other story is told merely to appease the Helmsdotterians. The flowering of the palm lilies was just an exceptional coincidence. Now, do you see why your being here is an issue?"

My jaw dangled open as I gasped understanding. "Ah, you assume that my presence here will cause the same thing to happen again? That's preposterous. I'm not that same boy! I still don't know why I should believe you."

The seer nodded. "I am most certain of it. The Were-fish my grandchildren slew was the first I have seen myself, but I recognized it immediately. I knew it from paintings given to me by the last Seer, my own grandmother. One does not forget the visage of something so terrible. It was coming after you, boy. You are the one the Were-beasts want."

"But, what am I to do? I can't leave the Island. I have no means! Even if I did, I don't know where I would go! I don't know who I am or where I'm from. You're asking me to commit suicide!"

"Well, what have you got to lose? A few days of consciousness? Some sweet memories of a girl who might fancy you? Seems a fair price to pay for the lives of innocent bird-folk and their families."

"That's not fair!"

"Fairness is irrelevant to my point. If you stay on this colony, you will bring a season of tragedy. You cannot risk Vespa's safety for your own sake, let alone the sanctuary of all my people. It's not acceptable! You must leave this place first thing tomorrow morning, and you must leave the girl behind. She will remain safe here."

"You aren't listening to me!" I pleaded. "I can't leave! There's no way I can get off the Island. I have to stay or I will die. If I'm stuck in this unfamiliar place, I'm going to stick with Vespa. She's the only familiarity I have. You can't deny me that!"

"Oh, can't I? I figured you would be unconvinced," Seer sighed. "If you care for her, you would do well to let her stay. However, there is yet something you can do. It will carry much risk. You and your friend might perish. Are you sure you can risk her well-being so casually?"

"Tell me what I can do."

"It's quite simple, really. Journey into the Mists and banish the Were-beasts from the land. Defeat those monsters and eradicate their ilk from the fabric of time. Not until then will you be truly welcome to stay in our halls."

"How am I supposed to commit this genocide? What weapons can I use to defeat an army of born hunters?"

"If I knew the answer to that riddle, we wouldn't be in this situation, would we? But, fear not, young Wingless. There is hope, if you believe. You must journey to the apex of Azure Peak and speak to the Phoenix. She may know the means you require to defeat the Were-beasts. She may also be able to answer some of your other queries."

"So, basically, you're sending me away on a wild goose chase?"

"Ha, if only that were the case. Wild geese are a honk and a half! This is much more straightforward. It's but a one-way journey to the answers you seek. But, the one way is away from here."

"Well, why haven't you gone to the Phoenix yourself?"

"And leave the safety of this colony? You overestimate my bravery, child. I have seen the Were-beasts do terrible things. I have no desire to experience any of that again."

"You could just be telling me lies just to get me off your pyramid."

"Well, you could always just leave the Island instead. Go, swim away and find another place to stay. Or, give in to the Weres and let them devour you whole. Whatever you do, you can't stay here. Just remember, you don't have to endanger Vespa's life. You should think long and hard about your decision. The correct decision may not be as clear-cut as you are thinking. Just make sure to choose by the morning. I will be making sure you leave no trace of yourself behind. I can take no chances with the safety of my people!

"However, this is a day for celebration, it would do more harm than good to send you away in the middle of Palm Sunday festivities. No, there's no reason we should cause concern among the other colonists. Tonight, try to enjoy yourself. The broiled Were-fish with rumbly sauce is supposed to be divine."

I thanked Seer and took my leave, burdened by the new knowledge of my doom-bringing. Stepping into the hallway, I found Vespa waiting. She tapped her foot while a concerned furrow rested furtively in her brow.

"I suppose you heard most of that," I offered.

"You're damn right I did," she replied. "You're not going anywhere without me, understand? For some reason, I feel like it's my fault you're here in the first place. If you go, I go. Gosh, we should have stuck together after the orchard. I'm going to leave Helmsdotter with you, no matter what."

"No, that's not true. I don't blame you a tic for this. I'm the one who's causing the Were-beasts to appear. For some reason."

"You don't even know that's the truth!" Vespa shouted. "I just showed up recently, as well. Maybe they're after me! The point is we don't know the whole reality of the situation, and we won't unless we talk to this Phoenix thing. Together, we're much more likely to survive until we reach the mountaintop. Capice?"

The girl knew how to warm a boy's heartcockles. "I'm grateful, really, but I can't ask you to come with me."

"You're not asking me, I'm telling you! End of discussion." She paused for a second. "I'm sorry, Charlie."

"What? No, you don't need to be sorry for anything."

"But, I need to apologize for the way I've been acting. I'm losing bits of myself, and it's scary. I don't know how you did it, waking up without a clue to guide you in any direction. You didn't know anything! Nothing at all! I'd probably have just drowned myself, right off the bat. And, I want to apologize for snapping at you. Maybe I really did say that I couldn't swim. Maybe I really said that I fell out of an airplane. I don't know the truth of the situation from the lies of the Island. So, I'm sorry."

I blushed, flattered and frightened. However, Vespa didn't give me a second to speak.

"Anyhow, I just needed to quick get that off my chest. But, get yourself excited, because it's time to celebrate! Come on, this way!" The mercurial maid grabbed my wrist and tugged me down a new hallway that looked eerily familiar. "Since we're special guests, we have primo treatment awaiting us at tonight's entertainment."

We traveled down another complex series of unremarkable hallways, indistinguishable to my eyes. We made at least a dozen turns before Vespa stopped. She opened one of the plain-and-tall doors and took my hand. We stepped through the threshold together and drowned beneath cheers from a crowd of reveling bird-folk on a panoramic balcony.

Quinn and Beverly waddled over and ushered us into the party, introducing us to some of their friends. Another albatross couple had come with their children, barely ten weeks old and still larger than me. One svelte, white lovebird pretended to be amiable while she sipped on a purple drink and sighed into her downy breasts. A lone, speckled booby brought over a plate of hors d'oeuvres, crab-steaks on crackers. He attempted to chat up Vespa while she snacked on his dish but, with some fancy footwork, we managed to sneak away to the main buffet table. The table was covered in a vast array of snacks and drinks. Bubble nuts and cocoa gum moistened my tongue at first sight. Pitchers of fizzy pops and salads tossed with edible petals flagrantly snared me with their fragrance. Purple, white, yellow, and red meats glistened on platters around a much larger, pink mound of flesh.

"There's no way I'm not eating a piece of this Were-fish," I shouted, drunk on the party's atmosphere. "Not after all the trouble it gave me!"

Vespa agreed. "I could even go for some rumbly jelly, straight from the jar."

We each filled a plate full of the sour sauces and savory meat, and then ate our fill at the rail of the terrace. Looking over the edge of the balcony was like dropping off the edge of the world. The pyramid was almost as tall as the Ring, and we stood close to the top. The water below was as dark as the sky above, but filled with giant, glowing flowers. The electric green and sultry purple blossoms skated across the surface of the lake below, like orbiting comets. They seemed to dance to the music, a concerto for string quartet played by a group of three albatrosses and a flamingo that couldn't stop bobbing in time with the beat. As I watched the flowers dance, I detected their aroma in the air. Difficult to describe, it smelled like home. Of course, that scent was a lie.

Senses saturated, I couldn't help but be riddled by joy. All my worry bubbled away as I sipped on a cankleberry fizz. I watched birds dance with their partners and friends, faces riddled with pleasure. A lanky lovebird, drunk on something potent, stumbled about whispering sweet nothings at playful chicks that, in turn, flirted with some gallant boobies. I was sad I couldn't call this wonderful place home. But, I decided that if my departure would protect this sphere of happiness and harmony, I would gladly leave.

As the night wore on, Vespa and I found ourselves sitting on the edge of the balcony, kicking our feet at the dangerous drop. Some albatrosses toted away the music and food as the festivities shifted gears to the final event. The other Helmsdotterians settled in and simmered down in anticipation of the grand finale. As the party slowed, so did my mood.

"So, this island that we've found ourselves on," I began, whispering in Vespa's ear, "The Island that we have no means of escaping, no possible method of understanding, it's absolutely terrifying, isn't it?"

Vespa laughed away my gloomy words. "Yes, silly. But don't you think it's kind of lovely, too?"

She leaned over and pecked my cheek as the first of many fireworks spiraled into the dark night sky.

I think the show was nice, but all I can remember is that the stars shined especially bright that night.

MELODY

The next morning, before we could do anything about the situation, Vespa and I were shuttled toward the exit of the colony. I woke bouncing on the back of an albatross waddling at mach speed through another familiar tunnel. It looked the same as every other tunnel I'd seen in the Colony, and my cognitive processing unit was running so slow I couldn't even begin to guess my position. Vespa's magenta mop was bobbing in front of me as she attempted to straddle the back of another bird. I recognized her dark steed as Quinn when Beverly's sweet voice vibrated up through my belly.

"Sorry to do this to you so brusquely," she said, "But Seer was quite adamant about getting you both off the grounds before sunrise. She wouldn't give us a reason for it, but then, she doesn't really need one."

"But don't worry none," Quinn's cotton speech echoed back to me, "The two of us are going to see our friends off safely. Yes, sirree!"

"Our little babies are going out to the big, big world," Beverly said. "I know you'll do us proud! Our little champions!"

I attempted to give my thanks, but a groggy throat combined with my vehicle's vibrations to distort my speech into a murky mumble. Vespa turned and offered me a vicious grin and a haughty toss of her hair. Keeping myself attached to

84

Beverly's shoulders was difficult enough without the burden of trying to hide my embarrassment.

I didn't have to struggle for long. The albatrosses made a quick turn and we spilled onto the colony's shores. Though the skies still lay dark, a powerful light fluoresced from the palm lilies still skating about the lake's surface. The sudden brightness was accompanied by a roar of applause, flowing from the eager wings of most of Helmsdotter's residents. I saw many familiar faces from the gala of the night before. Seer was notably absent.

"What's going on here?" I asked. "What is everybody doing?"

"Duh, silly," Quinn said, "We brought everyone out so they could have a chance to say farewell to their heroes!"

Deep inside my awareness, I felt a nascent mote of dread begin to multiply. I glanced at Vespa, whose usual playful facade had been replaced by a wince of embarrassment. The beaks of the bird-folk around me dangled in half-open smiles, as if they expected a grand speech from us noble apes. I didn't know how to address the situation, so I chose to ignore my audience for a moment.

"Vespa, do you know what this is all about?" I whispered.

The girl's cheeks flushed to match her locks. "I, I," she stuttered, "I may have had a little bit too much cordial last night. I also might have been a bit to forward in announcing our plans to, well, just about everybody." She shrugged. "Oops."

I sighed. I should have expected as much from the girl who couldn't even remember how she gotten to the Island. I turned my attention back to the congregation of admirers inching closer.

"Listen, all of you," I started. "I'm not sure exactly what you heard, but-"

"You're going to save us all from the Were-beasts!" a tiny, yellow fuzzball peeped as it fluttered, unable to control its avian energy. "You're gonna kill 'em dead!"

"Well, um," I said, startled. "I mean, that might happen, potentially, if-"

"The day of our liberation draws near!" the flamingo bandleader squawked.

A pair of perky boobies danced in a circle, touching by the tips of their wings. "Freedom! Freedom! We can go back home at last!" they chimed together. "What a magnificent day!"

Another chorus of applause and huzzahs drowned out any chance I might have had for rebuttal. The colonists swarmed forward and drowned Vespa and me in feathery hugs and kisses. Many of the birds tried to offer us assorted gifts or treasures. Some swallows filled my bowl with a cornucopia of vegetables and cheeses, to ensure we would not hunger. Under friendly duress, we also accepted less useful treasures, like the flamingo's violin, a swan's vanity mirror, and more birdseed than we could ever want. The whirlwind of gratitude lasted for several minutes, or an hour; the awkwardness of the situation overwhelmed my sense of time.

"Stop this nonsense!" a dramatic voice boomed from the Colony's threshold. Seer had deigned to make an entrance before our exit. "The sun is about to poke its nose above the crater's lip. If those two champions," she hissed, with not a little bit of spite, "Are not off this pyramid before I see the first speckle of dawn, there will be consequences the likes of which will spawn nightmares for years to come. Your children's children will remember the horror!"

The seething throng of admirers acquiesced, stepping away and quieting their fervor. However, their hopeful eyes never left our faces.

"Well," Seer continued, glaring at me through rheumy eyes. "Get going." She gestured at the crowd of her peers. "You have a lot of people to disappoint."

I packed up my pride and my hero's bounty and remounted Beverly's shoulders. Under a stifling tide of silence, Vespa and I departed. Our albatross friends zoomed across the lake's surface, weaving around some rogue palm lilies. I breathed deep to calm my nerves. The scent of the lilies whirled through my nose straight to my brain. That odd odor imprinted its sense of home, a feeling I had barely begun to understand.

We crossed half the lake's surface before sunlight began to sneak into the basin. As Beverly and I glided past a lackadaisical purple lily, I peered inside for a closer look. At the very center of the flower was a strange yellow button. This part of the flower alone emitted no fluorescent aura. Squinting my eyes, I saw a pattern on the button's surface that reminded me of a human face. I laughed to myself as the flower drifted back toward the pyramid. The home where I was no longer welcome. Though I convinced myself that it was a trick of the burgeoning light, as spinning petals obscured the face, I saw the button's eyes flash open to reveal lonely black orbs.

Quinn and Beverly left us on the shore with our small pile of gifts from the colonists. They gave each of us wet, fishy hugs before diving back into the tepid waters. Vespa and I found ourselves alone on the tip of a short peninsula. A short distance beyond the end of the sandy shore, a forest started and continued all the way to the inner edge of the Ring. Though the flora outside the crater wall was soft and inviting, the plant life in this jungle appeared sharp and repellant. I was not at all excited about diving inside. The mote of dread in my stomach had expanded into a full-fledged tumor of disconcert.

"That was a bit uncomfortable," Vespa said, avoiding eye contact.

I nodded. "Yeah. I've never been so glad to escape a crowd in my life. As far as I remember."

Vespa rolled her eyes, exasperated by something I had or hadn't said or done. "Well, we're out of the lake's sanctuary, so we'd best make the most of it. Unless you'd rather get eaten by Were-beasts, that is. I suggest we just start moving and don't stop until we get caught or miraculously find the Phoenix. But first, we need to decide what to do with all this-oh!" Vespa dashed over to a patch of reeds just beyond the tide line and rummaged around inside the foliage. "I can't believe it!"

She emerged dragging a large brown suitcase. "It's my father's luggage! Oh, Charlie! He must be nearby, maybe somewhere in the forest. Gosh, I guess we fell out of an airplane after all. Man, this Island sure has a mean effect on a girl's memories."

I ran over and put my hand on Vespa's shoulder, though she shrugged it away. "That's fantastic! You're right, he's probably somewhere in the forest. We'll keep an eye out for him while we explore it, okay? But we've got to start moving or the Mist will trap us here on the shore." I glanced over at the brambly mess standing between our destination and us. I couldn't shake the feeling that these plants didn't want us straying into their turf.

"Yeah, I guess that's probably best," Vespa murmured. "Let's fit as much of that food as possible into the suitcase. Then you can finally get rid of that silly bowl you've been carrying about."

"But, I like my bowl," I said. "It's been a good friend to me."

Vespa shook her hands with exasperation. "Fine. Whatever. Just help me clear out my father's clothes so we can fit in more of this cheese. And, find yourself an outfit more fitting of an adventurer."

"You don't like my clothes?"

"Oh, they're fine if you're an alcoholic suburbanite, but we're about to traverse who knows how many miles of nettles and burrs. Find something a bit more practical, all right? I don't want you getting hurt and whining every step of the way."

A frown frozen on my face, I spelunked through Vespa's father's clothing. After a few minutes, I was able to find a pair of heavy, blue jeans and an orange flannel shirt, both of which suited me to the nines. The garb made suitable armor for shimmying through sharp foliage.

"How do I look?" I asked.

Vespa glanced up from her game of intimate arrangements. "Like, maybe you won't die after thirty seconds in the woods. Nice work, master lumberjack."

"It's a bit odd, isn't it? Your father's clothes fit me perfectly. I have no clue who I am, and your memory has proven a little bit fuzzy. You don't think, maybe-"

"You are not my daddy," Vespa interjected. "No way, no how. Damn it, Charlie, you can be so dumb sometimes. I can't believe I'm following you on an expedition into no-man's-land. It's a good thing I'm a smart woman. Here, take this. I fit everything inside."

She tossed me the packed suitcase. It felt much lighter than it should have, considering how many sacks of birdseed, foods, and trinkets had been stuffed inside it.

"And how do I look?" Vespa asked, striking a coy pose. She placed my bowl on her head like a helmet.

"You would make a lovely acorn, miss. Or perhaps you would be a mushroom princess?"

Vespa shrugged off her blanket of invisible scorn and shook her head, keeping the bowl balanced. "Let's get going, silly boy. I don't want to get caught by the Were-beasts tonight or ever."

As the sun began its flaming parabola across the sky, we slipped into the shade of the forest. Instead of finding shelter from the heat, we met burning resistance. The plant population was stocked with a full arsenal of whetted blades. One type of succulent grew long, slender leaves with blood red tips coated by a mild poison. They inflamed my fingers moments after their touch. To make matters worse, they grew everywhere, poking us all day.

"Shit!" Vespa cursed. "Another bloody cut from another bloody leaf. What the hell, Charlie? Aren't you supposed to be a gentleman of some sort? Protect me, already!"

"You could try on some of your father's clothes, you know. We still have most of them." I had tried making this suggestion several times already. I knew her response before it came spilling out of those scarlet lips.

"I've already told you, no. I can't. Those are my father's clothes. It wouldn't be right."

"But it's all right for me to wear them? Why is that again? Hmm?"

"Because you're an idiot, just like him!"

Variations on this conversation repeated over and over during our trek. Vespa's stubbornness and irritability increased the temperature beyond its already incredible heights. As the sun approached its zenith, the moisture in the plants and ground around us began to evaporate. Vapors accumulated beneath the thick canopy to create a hellish sauna. With the rising heat increased our delirium.

"So, do you think we're lost yet?" I asked.

"God, do you have to complain about everything?" Vespa snapped. "Shit! That's got to be the hundredth slice on my leg. Damn, it burns! I swear, Charlie, if I die, I'm going to come back and murder you. Just shut up already. You're distracting me."

"Oh, distracting you? From what? Have you got some noble purpose, hmm? What makes you so special? Just what is with you today? I've been trying to offer you help and you've done nothing but attack me. What's going on?"

"Ugh," she grunted, "Never mind. I don't want to talk about this right now. We're on a quest, remember? To save the colony? Remember your promise to Quinn and Beverly and the rest of them?"

"Hey! That's not fair. I never promised anyone anything. If I remember correctly, another certain someone revealed our plans to the whole world. You probably claimed that we would kill the Were-beasts and then bring everybody bags full of presents. Is that what you did?"

"Oh, nice. Try and pin this on me, will you? It's your fault that we got exiled from Helmsdotter, anyway. You're the one the Were-beasts want. I'm just coming with you, tagging along for the ride. I could go back to that pyramid right now and have a fine fish dinner. Is that what you want? I will leave you, Charlie, if you're not careful."

I was shocked. "I, no, that's not what I want, Vespa. What is this is all about? You seemed so keen to come with me last night! What happened since then? Why are you so bitter about coming with me on this admittedly foolish quest? Am I doing something wrong? Are we going the wrong way?"

"No, that's not it," she exclaimed, with a pound of desperation. Before she could clarify what it actually was, we escaped the forest. The tension that had accrued between us crumbled away as soon as a cool breeze swept across our brows. The only remainder of our quarrel was a thin layer of salt all over our bodies, a memory of our sweaty battle. We stepped from the brambly woods into a large open clearing. It might have once been a meadow, but it was barren. Not a single blade of grass grew in the loamy soil, but a tremendous statue was poised at the center of the oval. I recognized it at once.

"That's a falcon. A mighty big falcon." Gasping for breath, I realized where we had stumbled. This statue marked the lost home of my lost companion, Downy.

"Very good," whispered a voice next to my ear. "You should consider ornithology."

I stumbled forward, scrambling to get away from whomever had the nerve to startle me. My face hit the soft dirt. A delicate but heavy foot pinned me to the ground. My foe was precise, yet powerful. I could see Vespa backing away, edging along the statue's dais.

"Well, well, little mite. I've heard so much about you, it's about time we met." My captor's voice had a raspy edge, as though his breath was air released from an exhumed coffin. I craned my neck to get a better look, but glare hid his identity.

"Who are you?" I gasped, my lungs halfway crushed.

"How rude of me to skip my own introduction. My name is Lucien, and I am Master of the Mists." My stuttering shock was muffled as Lucien continued speaking. "The Pharaoh of Fog. The Sultan of Steam."

"The Warlock of Weres?" Vespa asked.

"Oh, yes, I rather like that one," Lucien replied. "I like your style."

"Are you here to hurt us?"

"No, I'm merely here to proved some insightful metaphysical metacommentary as you traverse my little part of the metaverse."

"Really?"

Lucien laughed. "No, not really. I'm here to devour your scrumptious little souls."

"Step off my trophy, you filthy animal!" A squawk echoed through the clearing. "I'll slice you up and serve you for second breakfast." I could barely make out a brown figure poised for battle on the wing of a giant version of itself. Downy was alive!

Lucien internalized a deep hum of surprise, barely audible. "And who might you be, little bird? Certainly not somebody carrying a bone to pick with me? Oh my, how very terrifying."

A typhoon of feathers and battle squawks, Downy dove at Lucien. Whether it was intentional or not, I felt the grip of Lucien's heel loosen and I stole my chance to escape. I rolled out from under his weight and leaped to my feet.

Downy engaged a terrible beast in combat, a fierce juxtaposition of beauty and horror. Lucien's torso was that of a man like me, but embarrassingly fitter. His muscles rippled with every move, every twitch of his bones. His skin was smooth and pale, as though he had been carved from a glacier and animated by ancient sorcery. The chiseled features of his sullen face echoed this arctic sentiment, instilling him with a cold but pleasant aesthetic.

However, it was difficult to appreciate the Warlock's beauty without feeling a tinge of terror. From between Lucien's shoulders sprouted two wings, black and leathery, with a span at least twice as long as he was tall. As the sun lit them from behind, I could see dark, pulsing veins running through their webbing. His ears grew hard and gray, extending into horns that spiraled above his midnight locks. Worst of all were his eyes, empty sockets that seemed to absorb any light waves foolish enough to wander too close to their voids.

Though he appeared to be on the defensive, not returning any of Downy's attacks, Lucien was never threatened. He fought like he was teaching a dance. The Warlock led Downy into feints that would inevitably fail, just for the beauty of the motion. There was a strange game being played, and I couldn't quite understand the rules.

After several minutes of artful battle, Lucien leapt into the air with a laugh. His mammalian wings carried him up to the head of the falcon statue.

"Nice spirit, little bird, but I don't have the time to teach you any more fighting techniques today. I have an important audience with one of my subjects and must be leaving you for now. I just wanted to introduce myself, to let you know that I'm watching."

"Wait," Vespa asked, "You aren't going to try and take our souls?"

"Heavens no," Lucien chuckled. "No, ma'am. Rules are made for a reason, and there are rules that must be followed in this hallowed place. Isn't that right, little bird?"

"Get back down here, you cowardly cur!" Downy had begun to molt with rage.

Lucien laughed in reply, perched on the falcon's crest, before addressing me. "Charles, I don't believe you realize what you are getting yourself into. I know you're going after the Phoenix, hoping she might have some clues for you. You are hoping she might be able to help you to defeat me and my kind, but it's useless. She can offer you none of my weaknesses."

"Yeah, right," I scoffed. "Nice try. Also, it's Charlie."

"Oh, whatever. It's not like it will matter much longer. Look, I'll make you a deal. I swear," he said, "I won't even try to stop you from reaching her. She's got nothing on me. I'm untouchable. However..."

We waited in interminable silence, an awkward void that seemed to fuel Lucien's fiery grin.

"Yes?" Vespa asked. "However?"

"Okay, hear me out. It's not very exciting for me if I just crush you beneath my mighty magicks, so I'm willing to make a deal. I'm going to give you an opportunity to defeat me."

"And just why would you do that?" Vespa asked. "If you mean it, come right on down and I'll kick your face in."

Lucien laughed, falling into a fit of hysterics. "Gosh, you are by far my favorite! I'm not sure which of you should make me the most fearful. It's all a bit too much. And, no, girlie, I'm not going to just let you win. That'd be no fun for you. You've got to earn this one."

Something about this devil churned my guts. I wanted to slay him for Vespa, because he'd frightened her so. I wanted to crush him for Downy, for all the wrongs my friend had endured. I wanted to punch him in the kidneys for all the families he'd sent to the Colony.

"What's your game, scumbag?" I asked.

The Warlock smiled a grin that was just a hair too wide. "We're going to play Hide-and-Seek. Okay? I've taken something important to each of you and hidden it on the Island. If you find everything I've taken, I'll give you a weapon that just might be able to defeat me."

"I don't understand," I said, "This doesn't make sense."

"Oh no?" Lucien mock gasped. "It might seem a ridiculous premise for a game now, but I promise you'll be chuckling about how clever it was later."

"Yeah, whatever," Vespa spat, "It's not like we have anything important for you to take. We're stranded on this island, far away from our everyday lives. Besides, your secret weapon is probably 'friendship' or something equally lame."

"No, no, I have something much more explosive in mind. Something that'll rip me to pieces and then put me back together, just so it can tear me apart again. The best kind of weapon." Lucien shrugged. "Well, if you're not convinced, how about I give you a hint? Actually, I gave you a clue already, Miss Vespa, about what you have lost. But you had to go and put it in the hands of your clumsy companion."

Vespa's eyes darted to the luggage I'd dropped during the surprise attack. "Oh shit," she murmured. "My dad. You bastard! What did you do?"

Lucien stood, grinning, and took a short bow. "Thank you all for your time. You are such good sports. Isn't this much more exciting already? Yes, I think this is just what your adventure needed. A little drive, a little push! A-ha! I look forward to seeing you all again, very soon." With a grand flourish of his wings, Lucien vanished, leaving us in the shadow cast by the stony ghost of a falcon.

HARMONY

We sat in a circle of silence, each of us allowing hateful thoughts to consume our awareness. I felt like I was waking up from a nightmare, except the dream and reality were one and the same. My arch-nemesis had just exposed himself to me. I'd been granted the opportunity to end my quest without any further exertion. And yet, there had never been any chance of me defeating Lucien, Warlock of the Weres.

The man, if he could be called such, was much too powerful. It was all I could do to run and hide. First, I hid behind my friend's courage, then behind my shame. Unable to confront my companions or my self, I lay on my back and watched the sky burn away to a charred, shining black.

"Hey bird," Vespa said, breaking the heavy mood, "Thanks for trying to save us. Err, saving us, technically. I'm Vespa, by the way. It's nice to meet you."

"Hmm?" Downy muttered, surprised. "Vespa? That's a fine name for a prize. Oh, yes, you're a fine looking prize. You'll go quite well with my other trophy." He gestured to me. "A fine pair you'll make! A perfect set! You may call me Downy."

We spent the next hour or so swapping stories. Vespa and I explained the situation: our exile from the Colony, our quest for the Phoenix, and our need to defeat the Were-beasts by traveling through their home turf. Downy told us a terse, story about his last few days. He had awakened on the shore after abandoning me in the river. With the morning light illuminating his way, he had found his path back to the clearing. There he had spent the rest of his time hunting, unsuccessfully.

"The pigeons these days are just far too clever," he explained. "I try to snare them when they go all limp and statue-happy, but they're watching each others' backs. It's not fair."

"Downy," I asked, "What is this place? What happened here?"

"It's the ancestral home of kestrel-kind, the abode of falcon-folk. My family moved into this clearing before the brush grew green. When the Were-beasts came and slaughtered them in the night, I was still a hatchling. I had just learned to digest my own food! I had to bury all my kin, or, at least, what was left to be buried."

Vespa gasped. "Then, this loose earth..."

"Yes," Downy continued, "We are resting on the hundred corpses of my brothers and sisters."

Though it was but a brief flicker, I was able to catch the moment Vespa's heart broke. The sweet pixie transformed into a gnarled dryad, battered by years of loss and loneliness. She caught my inquisitive glance and put back her best smiling faerie mask. I could only smile back.

"I felt it fit to bury them here," Downy continued, "This is a place where a falcon could be proud to lie forever. Also, there isn't much of a better grave marker on the Island." He gestured to the noble sculpture at the center of the clearing. "The statue was cast by my father, the great artisan. It's a self-portrait."

Vespa put her hand out to ruffle Downy's feathers. "If his son is half the bird he was, then this statue isn't near big enough to capture his greatness. Still, it's an excellent memorial for a tremendous family."

Downy pretended offense at Vespa's touch by jumping away and muttering to himself, but something beyond his body language spoke verses of gratitude. His aura had been tweaked by Vespa's magic. He was flattered by her tribute to his family and his self, but was too full of pride to admit it. "I'm sure my father would say thanks or something," was all he said.

Vespa made a tiny pout. "I hope my father gets to say anything at all," she whispered. "I hope we find him. I just want to see him one last time."

"So, now what's the plan?" I asked, intent on saving our party's jubilant mood. I unpacked some food and cordial from Vespa's luggage. Hunger never solved any problems. "How do we start the process of kicking that jerk Warlock's perfectly chiseled ass?"

Vespa mauled a hunk of sweet cheese, chewing it deliberately. "He is really something, you know. The nerve of that guy, throwing us headlong into this stupid game! And involving my family, no less! I want to prove him wrong and beat the crap out of him. We've got to find his weakness!"

"I suppose I do owe you some sort of thanks," Downy said, devouring beakfuls of birdseed from the colonial offerings. "After all, you saved me the trouble of tracking down your partner trophy. No extra effort, and I've got the complete set. Maybe I can take you part of the way to complete your mission. At least, I can get you started."

"So, you'll take us to see the Phoenix?" Vespa pleaded, beggar eyes lit by the orbiting moon.

"Yeah, I suppose I can show you the way. I've got to follow along, you know. I'm not risking the chance that another bullheaded fool might hurt either of you and ruin my perfect trophy pair, just after I've found both of you."

Vespa smiled a bright moonbeam to cut through our gloomy night. It was easy to see that the falcon's cold affection had warmed her heart as much as she had tweaked his. "But of course, noble hunter. And, of course, we can find out what the old Warlock has taken from you and begin our quest for vengeance. If you think it's worth your time, of course."

Downy nodded and muttered agreement. "Tonight," he said, "We should stay here, where it's safe. Tomorrow, we'll start for the Azure Egress, a pass carved into the Ring by some vigilant mountainfolk. It's quite well hidden, but I know the way, my Father used to take me up to the mountains now and then. The Egress leads all the way to the Azure Peak. We can make it to the cliffs in one day if we leave first thing in the morning."

"Is it really safe here?" Vespa asked. "This place is wide open. There's no cover, no defense. How's it safe here?"

"Lucien wasn't lying about him being unable to attack us here. It's hallowed ground. The Mist can't destroy the same place twice. It's one of the rules, like 'Mist can't spread over water' and 'Mist can't rise above 1500 feet.' It's easier to accept when you've seen the Mist suddenly stop it's pursuit. Right, Charlie?"

I agreed with him. It was strange, but I'd seen the Mist stop a relentless assault at close quarters, for no better reason than because it had hit water's edge.

"Okay, that explains why the Weres are stuck on the Island," Vespa said. "Their foggy home can't swim across the ocean or fly away. So, why don't people just move into hallowed ground? Why isn't everyone living up in the mountains where it's safe?"

Downy shook his head. "Look at the ground around us. It's fallow earth. Nothing will grow in this ground. Plants will not tarnish the souls of the dead, they know better. Also, can you imagine living here, where pieces of corpses are buried a few feet below your toes? Some people do move up to the mountains, but not many. Once you meet some of the mountainfolk, you'll understand why others are a little bit reluctant to move there."

"Why's that?"

"Let's just say that living on a mountain leads to some interesting, alternative lifestyles."

Vespa nodded, as if this were the most logical statement in the world. I imagined a constant, crazy gala with loud music and lots of wigs. It bothered me that these imaginary mountainfolk lived life unconcerned by the double-threat of avalanches and rockslides.

"Well, okay," Vespa said, "That seems easy enough. We find the pass, climb the mountain, and find the Phoenix. And then, we ask our questions and continue on to the next stage of our quest. Right?"

"Sure, sure," Downy said, unconvinced. "But, as with the Mists, there are Rules for the Phoenix."

"Go on," I goaded.

"For example," Downy said, "There is a tribe of mountainfolk who won't let anyone in to see the Phoenix until they've proven their worth."

"Oh, good," Vespa moaned. "I'm glad the Phoenix is well protected."

"And," Downy continued, "Those persons who are able to pass the trials of worthiness are allowed to ask no more than two questions of the all-knowing bird."

"Double-fudge-dipped rumblies," Vespa cried.

"I don't think that's so unreasonable," I reasoned, "Information is a valuable commodity. The Phoenix can't just go about giving answers to anybody and everybody. Besides, we've got a brave falcon, a clever girl, and a, well, I've got a good bowl."

My companions nodded their assent.

"It's a very nice bowl," Vespa added, tracing its inner lip. "I've come around. I think I understand why you kept it close."

"I wonder what questions I should ask," I said. "Should I try to find out what I'm missing? Should I ask where to look for it and just try to find it when we get there? Or should I go for the glory and just ask about Lucien's weakness? That guy's got something coming for him!"

"Tell me about it! He kidnapped my father," Vespa said, "I just know it. I'm just going to find out where that bat-bastard took my pops and then go bust his rodent face to a pulp. So, that gives me an extra question. I can ask about his weakness."

Downy leaned on the machete, emitting a facade of nonchalance. "He's already taken my family from me. There's nothing I've got left that means anything to me. He can keep whatever it is for all I care. No matter what, I'm going to murder him and mount him on my wall. He's not worthy of the wings on his back. I'll ask where we can find this sacred weapon and how we can use it to kill him."

Satisfied by our plans, excited by thoughts of revenge, we agreed it was time to rest before our journey in the morning. Downy clambered up between the statue's legs to sleep. I wanted to talk with Vespa about whatever it was that was nagging at her, but she vanished before I got the chance. Half-worried about her safety, half-exhausted by our trek, I passed out on a soft patch of earth. Like the falcons six feet below me, I was dead to the world.

The three of us set off at dawn. Downy took point while I guarded our rear, dragging Vespa's suitcase through the underbrush.

We slipped through the forest at a rapid pace. The only sounds were moist swishes of branches against our bodies and the occasional "shit" from Vespa as she acquired another scar. The Mist had cleared all fauna out of the jungle, but these plants harbored plenty of dangers on their own. Still, Vespa refused to wear any of her father's clothes. I found myself unable to be bothered by her stubbornness; I was much too busy being plagued by terrible visions. The morning light birthed undulating shadows everywhere I looked. The moving darkness tricked my mind, teasing me with half-glimmers of hungry beasts or watchful eyes that I knew, logically, weren't present. For half a moment, I believed I was still dreaming, asleep on the loam.

I imagined Lucien stalking us on our journey, waiting for us to let down our guard and devour us. I wondered if his silly game and his promise to allow us safe passage to the Phoenix were just subtle tactics, cheap ploys to trick us into lowering our defenses.

Though time was passing, the sun seemed fixed at an angle that maximized its efficiency at heating the earth. We had embarked before morning light, but the air grew thick with sweat and steam. I felt my blood thin, and I grew more irritable by the second.

"Downy," I asked, "How much further do we have to trek? I'm tired."

"Honestly," he said, "I have no idea."

"What? You promised you could take us to the Phoenix!" Vespa yelled, her temper running on steam power. "This is your home turf! Do you have any idea where we are?"

"Well, I've been looking for a certain landmark to direct us, a small pond with a rock in the middle that looks like a drowning albatross. I expected we would find it about an hour ago. We're supposed to make a turn toward the Azure Egress there."

"And what was your plan for if we missed the turn?" Vespa asked.

"Oh, I wasn't planning on missing it," Downy said.

"What you're saying is that we're totally, hopelessly lost," Vespa moaned. "What you mean to say is that we're going to find ourselves trapped in the middle of nowhere when night falls, and the Were-beasts will be able to munch us up like a sack of candied meats."

"No, no," Downy relented, "I'm sure my sense of time is just a little bit off. We'll find the Drowning Pond soon enough, and then it's just a few hours more until we reach the Ostrich Boulder. The Azure Egress is only another hour after that. I'm confident we'll reach the safety of altitude by nightfall."

Four hours later, fate found us still wandering around the forest, unable to find any tangible landmarks. We never found any random clearings in our path, so we never left the uncomfortable atmosphere of boiling foliage, never allowed our tempers to simmer down. Hardly a word passed between us that wasn't a complaint or outright insult. I prayed the air would begin to cool, marking the beginning of the sun's descent behind granite blinds. At least when the Mists came to swallow us up, they would bring relief from the heat.

Before hope wore through its last threads, Downy shouted with joy. "There! Up ahead, I see fresh air. We've found it, we've found the first landmark!"

The three of us dashed toward our goal. Vespa sprinted into the lead, protecting her face from harm with my stalwart bowl. I lagged behind, burdened by her father's luggage. I was far enough behind that I could watch my friends' reactions upon their exit from the woods. Vespa's shoulders fell and she dropped my bowl. Downy plopped his bird-butt onto the ground as though his gravity had doubled. These were not symptoms of chronic jubilation, but acute defeat. As I stepped from the

109

woods into the failing light, I was caught by their same affliction.

In the middle of the clearing we stumbled into was a giant statue of a falcon. Despite a day of hard travel, we had gone nowhere at all.

DISCORD

"At least we're safe," I jested, trying to lighten the dusky mood. "No souls will get eaten tonight!"

Neither Vespa nor Downy felt up to laughing, or even acknowledging my lame attempt at humor.

"I don't understand what happened," Downy said. "I've made this journey so many times before, I can't imagine what went wrong this time."

"Don't worry yourself," I said, "I'm sure Lucien is messing with us. I knew he was lying when he said he would let us visit the Phoenix unhindered. That jerk was leading us on. He's probably having a grand old laugh right about now."

"Also," Vespa said, "He's doing something terrible to my father. There are a lot of things you can do to harm a person in a day."

"I'm sorry!" Downy squawked, pacing. "If it were up to me, we would be in the mountains right now, discovering the secrets of our nemesis' weakness. Quit breaking my beak!"

"Okay, fine," Vespa said, "But what about tomorrow? What happens then? Will we be able to make it to the cliffs? Or will this happen again and again? Like a record on repeat, we'll be stuck humming the same word over and over. That word, of course, being: 'shit'. Shit! Shit! Shit!"

Downy started to molt again. "Don't forget, pretty thing, that you are my trophy and I am only taking you to the Phoenix out of the goodness of my heart. I could just take you home and mount you."

"I'd like to see you try!" Vespa snarled.

"On my wall!" Downy gasped. "I meant on my wall. I would never, I mean, of course you are a perfectly lovely girl, but that's just disgusting. I just want you to know, I'm doing this because I'm trying to care about the safety of my possessions."

"And also because of your thirst for revenge," Vespa slipped.

"And," Downy continued, "Because I am a great hunter worthy of acclaim. I am after my greatest quarry ever, no disrespect to either of you. If he is trying to stymie my progress, it proves him to be worthier prey. Tomorrow, I will toss the die of fate and try again. We will succeed, I can feel it in my hollow bones!"

"Wait," I said, "Say that again. It sounded funny."

"I can feel it in my hollow bones?"

"No, before that."

"I will toss the die-"

"Bingo!" I said. "Something's wrong. Yes! You, as a great and noble falcon, should be casting the die of fate, should you not?"

"Oh shit," Vespa and Downy murmured together.

"Lucien took something from all of us," I continued. "Downy, do you think maybe he stole away your hunter skills? Your sense of direction and ability to trail blaze could be totally gone! Vanished."

"Oh, horsefeathers," Downy said, his color shifting from mud to khaki.

"That sneaky bastard," Vespa said, "He found a way to hamper us indirectly. He's not lying, not about any of it. He's taken something from all of us, but he won't stop us from reaching the Phoenix's lair. Now we have to find the Azure Egress another way, we can't rely on Downy's tracking sense any more. This is bad."

"Tell me about it," I said, "There's no way we can find our way to the Egress without Downy's knowledge and skill."

"What are we going to do?" Vespa asked. "We can't just stay here. I need to do something. I have to get moving, go find what has been stolen from us, rescue my family. Oh! This sitting around is making me crazy."

"Hey, we'll think of something. Just calm down for a minute," I said, gesturing at Downy. The falcon was hunched over in a curl of guilt, his feathers ruffled with emasculation.

"Oh, I didn't mean," Vespa started, "I'm just so worried about my mother, I can only imagine what Lucien is doing to her."

"You mean, you father? We don't know whether he has your mother or not."

"Well, we found my mother's suitcase in the reeds by the shore. So, I'm assuming he was referring to my mother when he mentioned giving me a clue."

"No, Vespa. We found your father's luggage. I'm wearing clothes that we found inside! I sure hope your mother and I don't have such similar figures."

Vespa squinted at me, her eyes screaming libel. "I see," was all she said.

With none of us able to voice constructive opinions, the conversation ended and we all went to sleep. I noticed, as my thoughts began to melt, two odd facts about our situation. For the second night in a row, I couldn't see where Vespa had wandered to for sleep. Also, there was no Mist surrounding us, trapping us in the glen. For the second night in a row.

My interest in these odd coincidences was stripped away by a particularly lucid dream. I wasn't even sure it was a dream, at first. My surroundings were all too familiar. I rushed through a corridor of emerald leaves, serrated brush cutting my legs to ribbons. An unfamiliar figure ran before me, leading me by my hand with a velvet grace. The stranger was garbed in a white, luminescent robe, his head covered by a hood. He appeared to be human, a beast without wings. I had a sense I might know him, but he would not turn his head to look back at me. Though we zoomed through the forest, my experience was more like floating through a transparent jelly. The images before me were not continuous, but flashed by a strobing projector hidden behind us.

We burst from the tree line and the stranger dropped my hand, rushing forward to greet the midnight colored wall a few yards away. He pressed his body against the azure barrier, dissipating its cool darkness with his hot aura. The solid rock melted away at his touch, dissolving until an infinite staircase remained. He took the first step up toward unfathomable heights, then turned and beckoned for me to follow. I couldn't step forward; I couldn't budge at all. The face of this specter was blank. It looked as though he wore a veil of shifting static. He gestured again, more urgently this time, that I should follow. When I struggled to find the resolve to lift my foot, I woke to a terrible din.

It sounded as though a hive of rabid hornets had descended upon us. I leaped to my feet and grabbed my bowl, the only object in arm's reach, to use as a weapon. I would ram my foes from behind the shield's protection, should it be necessary. After a bout of scattered confusion, I found the source of the commotion. Vespa sat a few yards away with the flamingo's violin, attempting to produce a simulacrum of an etude.

"What the devil are you doing?" I asked. "I was still sleeping!"

"Well, lazybones, I was just getting prepared for today's journey," she replied, "I figured if we were going to be lost again all day, we should at least have some music."

"If you can call it that," Downy moaned, "Look, she's already broken a string, just trying to tune the instrument."

"At least I'm trying to help the situation," Vespa snapped. "I'm making the most out of being trapped here with the two of you imbeciles."

"Hey!" I shouted, the fragments of my vision realigning in my subconscious processor. "I think I have an idea. Downy, do the plants stop short of the Ring on the inside, like they do on the outside?"

"Yeah," he admitted, "Why?"

"If we make it to the wall, can we just hug it tight and follow along the cliffs until we reach the Azure Egress?"

The simplicity of my plan struck Downy like a bolt of static. "Su-sure," he stuttered, "But it will take an extra half day of travel, at least. We'll probably have to camp out there, beyond our sanctuary. Don't you think that's too risky?"

"I don't think that the Mist is going to be a problem today. It didn't show either last night or the night before. I think Lucien is genuinely curious about whatever trouble we've stirred up. Something about us makes him worried. He doesn't understand it, so he's willing to wait a bit longer and see what develops. We should take this chance and go for it. There's no way we can get lost this time."

Downy nodded. "I think, no, I know we can get to the wall. If you're sure the Mist won't come, we can try it. If you're wrong, well, I don't have the hunter's skills to protect us. Not anymore."

"Vespa, what do you think?"

She was busy repacking her instrument. "Mist? No Mist? Either option sounds better than sitting around here waiting for a miracle. Let's get going."

We embarked after breakfast and hit the wall before midday hunger morphed us all into grouchy trolls. Just as expected, the forest plants stopped growing far from the stony face, giving us a corridor wide enough to walk down side-by-side. We made rapid progress and found some cheer, swapping jokes and singing some songs that none of us quite knew. For just a brief moment, life seemed as normal as normal might be for two humans and a falcon on a quest for a Phoenix. Everything flowed, as it should. It was all just fine until we made camp for the night, an immeasurable distance from the Azure Egress.

I dreamed of the faceless stranger again. I lay on my back beneath a tree with leaves of molten glass and limbs of river clay. I watched as the branches twisted about with wild abandon, whipping ever closer to my head. I could only move my face a little, only so far as to turn it left and right. Tilting my head all the way to the left, I managed to see the specter, looming. He stood, wearing the same glowing fashion statement, his arms extended wide. He thrashed about, like he was conducting the molten tree in an interpretive opera. I was so rapt by his hypnotic suggestions that I did not notice the branches' approaching. One white-hot shard scratched my shoulder and caused my world to fracture into six hundred continents of pain.

Vespa shook me awake with one finger pressed against her lips, one hand gripping my shoulder. Echoes of my dream pain reverberated beneath her fingertips.

"We need to talk," she whispered, "Don't wake Downy."

The bird who had so adamantly insisted on taking the first watch was fast asleep, his beak resting on his feathered chest.

I wiped the last molecules of sleep-state from the corners of my eyes. "What's up?" I yawned.

"Charlie," Vespa said, a set of parallel worry-lines crossing her brow. "I'm sorry, but I'm not coming with you any further. At least, not now."

"What are you talking about? We're just a day or two away from speaking to the Phoenix and answering all of our questions! Come on, if you don't scale the Azure Peak with us, you'll get caught by the Mists, before we're prepared enough to handle them."

"No, Charlie," she said, "You don't get it. I've been thinking about this for the last couple nights, and I'm sure it's what I need to do. I can't play about any longer. I must to go directly into the Mists."

"You can't be serious!"

"I'm certain that's where Lucien is keeping my mother. He's probably got whatever he's stolen from you in there, too. I'm going in, and I'm not coming out until I've gotten my family back to safety."

"All right, maybe you're on to something here. Maybe he's keeping our treasures close. He could be sending us off after a red herring and having a good couple laughs at our expense. You think you're going to be able to just waltz in there and take them back? Vespa, I don't think it works like that. He'll eat you up before you get anywhere near your dad! Or mom. Whoever! You're going to die! I can't bear to think about that."

"No, I'll find my mother. Lucien wants me to find her, for some reason. I don't know why, but I'm certain it's true. I think you are right. He's scared of something happening, something he doesn't understand. Something you and I and Downy are stirring up. Curiosity has gotten the better of him. Even if it kills him, he's got to understand this mystery."

"Well..." I started, knowing already that any argument would fall flat against Vespa's will. She had already made up her mind; there was no turning back up the mountain. "Well, then I'm coming with you. I'm sure Downy will agree, with a little persuasion. Maybe you're right. Maybe he's got our treasures, too. Look, Vespa, I can't just-"

"No, Charlie," Vespa interrupted. "No, I need to do this alone."

"But, you've got no weapons. No skills in combat."

"I'll think of something, if it comes to that. I don't think it will."

"Vespa, together we make such a team. When I'm with you, I feel... I don't know. Invulnerable. Apart, I know I will be powerless. This is exactly what Lucien is after, dividing us so we must fail."

A grimace flickered across Vespa's face. "Ugh, I hate your abuse of logic, Charlie. I need to get away, now. I'm sorry. I just, it's been too strange since that night. Doesn't it feel awkward to you?"

"What are you talking about?"

"You know, the night at the Colony? Haven't you thought about it much? Like, all the time? It happened only a few nights ago. You couldn't have forgotten already. And I you didn't drink a thing! You must remember!"

I could only remember intense sensations of pleasure: the oracular spectacle of palm lilies dancing, the savory delight of Were-fish in my mouth, the ethereal vibrations of the flamingo's quintet, and the transcendent tingle of Vespa's lips on my cheek.

"Oh," I blushed, "About that! I see what you're getting at. I mean, I was thinking about talking to you about it, someday. Maybe. I just hadn't found the right moment."

"Yeah, I wondered if you were going to apologize for taking advantage of my drunken state."

My jaw popped wide. "What are you talking about? That night? You kissed me! Right here on the cheek!"

"I do declare," Vespa's usually placid features began to ripple and flush. "That's not something I would do. I'm an honorable lady! And all these accusations! Jeepers, Charlie! I'm sorry. Maybe you're right. But, maybe you're wrong. Ever since we met, you keep telling me different stories than my memories tell me! I don't know what to believe anymore. I want to trust you, but there's already a truth in place up here," Vespa pointed to her brain. "Sometimes it seems like you're deliberately trying to confuse me! I don't know why, but damn if that isn't what it feels like."

"I swear! I'm not! It's the Island. It's confusing you!"

"I'm sorry, Charlie. I just need to get away for a bit and sort all this weirdness out. If you really care for me, you won't follow me. This is something that I must do for myself! I know we'll meet up again soon. It's a certainty. Trust in that, if you can. Who knows? Maybe, by then, we'll have found whatever it is we've lost. It might make all the difference in our friendship."

Vespa's magic was back in full effect. She paralyzed me once more, using a more drastic spell this time. I was bound tight with a caustic cobweb wrapped around my heart. Though she knew my jaw was wired shut by her craft, her eyes looked as if they were hoping for a response. I couldn't release a single syllable.

"Bye, Charlie. I'll see you soon."

Vespa loped into the trees, dragging her father's luggage behind. She left me with my bowl, filled with a little food but emptier than ever. Once beyond the brush line, Vespa was swallowed by the omnipotent shadows of midnight darkness. I collapsed back into a fetal position and spent the rest of the night failing to fall asleep, wishing I could somehow learn a counter jinx to the spells raining hard upon me.

COMPLEMENT

It took us the best part of another day to reach our goal, and not a word was said about the pink elephant missing from the room. The Azure Egress was even more impressive in real life than in my dream. It was a massive staircase, hewn into the inner cliffs of the Ring. Though the innermost edge lacked a wall or guide rail, the steps themselves lay wide enough to hold an entire marching band. They would be safe under normal hiking circumstances.

Downy and I scaled the ascent into the strange hours of the night, when dreams could blend with reality and subconscious thoughts might manifest themselves in strange forms. I imagined patterns on the rock face, subtle stories carved to relate our recent adventures to future hikers. I wanted to skip ahead, to get a spoiler about the ending of our journey, but instead I saw shades of the recent past. To quell my frustration, I looked to the stars and saw a waning half-moon, shining. This troubled me further. The lunar sliver was too much like the smile I already missed so much.

Downy was keen to pick up on my sad state. "We could go back and find her," he said. "Or help her find her father. The Phoenix will wait for us. In fact, the Phoenix probably already knows which day to expect us, so it doesn't matter what we do with our time before we arrive. "

"No," I said, "This is something Vespa must do for herself. She must find her own path to truth, and so must I. That's all there is to it. I should have seen it sooner."

"There's no reason you can't figure things out on your own, together."

"No, Downy, it's more complicated than that. I need to respect her decision. She's a smart girl and she knows what she wants. I think I can support it. Besides, we've come so far. No point in turning back now, right?"

"I'm no expert on Wingless relationships, but-"

"Just stop it, all right? Don't press me right now, okay. I'm fine. Vespa's fine. We'll all be fine once we complete this quest. And, what is that supposed to mean, anyway? Wingless? I've been hearing it thrown about a lot."

"You and that girl. You're Wingless. You don't have wings, see? It's pretty obvious once you stop to think about it."

"Yeah, but the way you said it was a bit demeaning."

"Well, I don't mean to offend you. It's just an old speech habit that comes out when I'm stressed. See, it's commonly believed that Wingless are less complete people than Winged. Personally, I think you are just fine, but others are less open-minded. I should warn you, the mountain folk might be a little bit backwards about this sort of thing. I don't think many Wingless make it up the slopes."

"There have been others? Why didn't you say anything?" I snapped. "How many have there been? Where are they now? They could tell me the things I need to figure out! They might know where I'm from and how I arrived here."

"I didn't think it was such a big deal. You're the first Wingless I've ever caught, so I'm not sure how to deal with your kind. Sorry. It's not like there are tons of humans running amok. I've just heard of a few in my father's stories. If you're so interested, you can always ask the Phoenix any questions you might have. Ask her all about the other Wingless, if you want."

I realized it was pointless to be mad at my remaining companion. He was only trying to help, after all, and I wasn't in a position to turn down any sort of aid.

"Thanks, Downy. I guess I'm still not quite used to the way things work around here."

"It's okay. The whole Wingless and Winged division is stupid and vain. Some people think that you have to have wings to be beautiful. The Phoenix is widely considered the most beautiful creature on the Island, as well as the most wise. She has perfect wings, if the rumors are true. So, obviously, you are the opposite of she. The supremest form of ugly. You just can't be beautiful if you don't even have wings."

I shrugged. "I guess that makes sense."

"Sugar, that's terrible logic," said an invisible speaker, whose voice was as soft as peach fuzz. "Oh, honey, you're so delicious I want to slice you up and put you in my sandwich."

I stopped walking and jumped into a defensive stance. "Did you hear that? Who's there?"

Downy continued up the steps. "I heard it, Trophy. It's best if you don't give it much thought. Just keep on walking and forget you heard anything."

I looked around for the source of the forehanded insult, but saw nobody on the steps. There was not a soul up on the wall, and nothing flying off the edge of the stairway. The statement could have come from anywhere.

"Yeah, okay," I said, continuing the climb. I was much too distracted to worry about an invisible echo. "Well, I didn't have any issues with the Winged folk of Helmsdotter. Just about everybody there treated me like I was family."

Downy scoffed. "People who have experienced tragedy are often more accepting of those who are different or odd. We look for hope and happiness wherever we can find it. That's is why I'm taking you on this silly quest instead of turning you into a glorious sculpture. Not that I'm not going to turn you into a sculpture later. I'm just honoring your last request, out of respect to your homeliness."

"Also, your revenge?"

"Yes, yes, I suppose. I mean, if Seer foresaw you defeating Lucien, I guess I should have a little faith in you."

"Also, to help Vespa?"

"Well, it wouldn't do to search for another Wingless partner to complete my set! You two make the perfect pair already."

I threw my hands in the air, exasperated. "I think so too!" Embarrassed by my lack of control, I tried to hide my emotions. "I mean, I thought that might be the case. We fit together like a pair of shoes. But, if that's true, then why did she have to leave?"

"Now you're upset she's gone?" came the mysterious voice. "I was right. You're so sweet I want to grind up your bones and sprinkle them in my tea!"

This time, the source of the voice was right behind us. I spun to find myself in front of the most striking bird-lady I'd ever seen. Her body was that of a feline, four-legged and coated by golden fur. Where a cat's head might have been was a woman's torso, bare as truth. The wings on her back were angelic, covered by white, downy feathers. Full breasts dangled over a taut stomach, lacking a belly button. Precariously placed strands of her hair, brown and sinewy, extended down to the short fur at her waist and just covered her nipples. The Winged woman's face was kind, its features soft and round. I might have been struck by a spell of lust had her eyes not been empty, black pits.

"Were-woman?" I asked. "W-w-w-w-"

The lady laughed. "Yes? I'm right here, sugar."

"Don't look at it," Downy said. "That's how they get you, these filthy Sirens."

"Hey now, dumpling, let's not get hostile," the Were-lady said, "I clean myself far more regularly than you, judging by the smell of your tailfeathers. You're so stinky I wouldn't even mistake you for a ripe horse fart."

"Not another word, vile hag," Downy growled. "Go back to the Mists where you belong."

"Master Downy," she said, "I'm so sorry for the trouble my people brought upon you. I can understand you might be upset at some of my brothers and sisters, but you know that I had nothing to do with the slaughter of your family. I'd left the Mists long before then, you know that!"

"Whoa, whoa," I said, stepping between the bristling brown featherball and his bizarre acquaintance. "You two know each other?"

"We've met before," Downy said before shutting his beak tight.

"Several times," the girl noted, "I'm Cheri Puckleblossom. I'm this little fellow's mother."

My brain stopped all its regular functions. It had broken some sort of integral thought gear; all processing power vanished with this calamity. I had no back-up generator, no replacement part. I was dead in the water of this stagnant conversation.

"Huh?" I inquired.

Downy sighed and began to mutter. "Your instincts were right, Charlie. When we first met, you thought it odd that I called myself a falcon. Well, I'm not exactly the falcon you might expect. I'm a half-breed. Half of a true hunter. And the reason is standing before us: my mother. This monster and my Father coupled during one of his jaunts up the mountain. She gave him my egg on his descent and I was raised as a pure falcon. It wasn't until she came looking for me almost a year after my birth that I was told of my sordid beginning.

"There is only one reason I was spared while my family was slaughtered. It was not because my so-called-mother did anything to stop it. Not because she gave us any warning. No, heaven forbid! That might have saved us all and spoiled her black heart. No, the reason I am alive is simply that the Were-beasts couldn't tell me from one of their own, so they never bothered to kill me. I must live on knowing my only saving grace is that I smell just like a fetid Were-beast!"

I wanted to go hold my brave companion, to tell him I cared. I understood now why he had overemphasized his heritage when we met. I knew why he tried so hard to compensate for his shortcomings. This ancestry was his secret shame. Instead, I left my body to its own devices and opened my mouth.

"Is this for real? Or, did I fall asleep? Downy, if Cheri left the Mists when she says, she couldn't have been responsible for your family's massacre. So, why do you hate her so?"

Downy scrunched himself tight, his feathers ruffled. "Once a Were-witch, always a Were-witch."

"Really now, honey, you aren't from around these parts," Cheri said, looking at me. "People like you and I, we're different. People don't like us. It might not seem fair, but a few bad seeds ruin it for those of us who've done nothing wrong. It's called prejudice."

"I don't understand. You're a Were-beast, a killer of innocents. It makes sense that people might be afraid of you, but what did the Wingless do to make everyone hate us?"

"It's simple," Downy grumbled, "Your kind has always been looked down upon, from the first days of Winged settlement on the Island. Time has passed but that fact hasn't changed. The Wingless have always and will always be viewed as less than complete people."

"Oh, but only by those people who are incomplete themselves," Cheri said, in a singsong voice. "Thanks goodness my child has the genetic fortitude to step beyond that shallow nature. Incidentally, whatever are you doing out in my part of the Island, Downy? Why didn't you call? I thought it would be ages before I would see you again."

"If I'd had my way, it would have been a long while yet before we met. I'm taking my friend to see," he paused, his voice uncertain, "We're going to the Kingdom of Town to get some creamed ice. Because he's new to the Island, I want to show him its finer qualities." He nodded to me. "Isn't that right, Trophy?"

I looked between Downy and Cheri, who both stared back at me with scrying eyes. Cheri seemed like a sweet enough bird-lady, but I had to trust my companion. "Yes, yes, of course. Downy's giving me a tour of the Island. The Kingdom of Town is our next stop. I do hear lovely things about the creamed ice."

Cheri nodded. "Oh, well, that's convenient! I'm headed there myself. I come out of my cave once a year, at least, so I can see the Kingdom Pageant. All the most beautiful birds of the mountain will be there, and I'm sure they've got some special flavors of creamed ice prepared for the occasion. Let's walk the rest of the way together!"

"Ha!" Downy laughed, as though this were the most ridiculous thing he'd ever heard. "You'd like that, wouldn't you? Trophy, a word." We walked a few feet away and began to whisper. Downy kept looking over my shoulder to make sure Cheri stood at a distance. "Trophy, no matter what nice things she says, no matter how pretty she may look, she's a Were-beast. We can't trust her. It's bad news if we let her tag along. Lucien said he wouldn't interfere with us, but that doesn't mean one of his minions can't."

I shrugged. "I don't know. It might be that you're overreacting."

"Overreacting!" he hissed. "To my family's massacre? You're out of your mind!"

I scrambled to correct my misspeak. "I mean, wouldn't it be better to have her close by, so we can keep an eye on her. If we let her go now, she might tell Lucien all about us. That is, if she's still a part of the Mist community."

Downy thought for a second. "Perhaps you're right." He shouted at Cheri, "Come on, Were-witch. We're moving now, but you'll have to keep up with our pace. We're not waiting on a Were."

I followed Downy as he continued up the steps and shook his head at Cheri. As I passed her by, she watched me with a slightly skewed smile stretched wide beneath her empty eyes.

SUPPLICANT

We walked onward and upward through the night, traveling an entire day without rest. I hadn't slept the night before, and was beginning to hallucinate. Downy refused to rest for fear our new companion might kill him in his sleep. He refused to talk for fear he might reveal a secret she could use against him. Cheri spent the time trying to know me better, asking me all sorts of questions that I didn't know how to answer with real words. Sleep deprivation was a harsh mistress.

The next day and night passed so smoothly that we didn't so much arrive at the Kingdom of Town as find ourselves in the middle of it. When the light of dawn crept over the lip of the Ring, it revealed that we had stumbled into the heart of a densely populated area. I counted dozens of homes, marked by holes in the rock face at the top of crudely carved ladders. Our party soon came upon a massive hole, at least ten times my height and width, on the level of the stairs. At the back of the hole, built into the Ring wall, was a grand portal. Two birds, one red, one black, stood guard and watched our approach.

"Halt!" the red bird cried, leveling his staff menacingly. "Who goes there?"

"Come forth!" the black bird replied, raising a sickle. "State your names and business!"

"Oh my, dears," Cheri said, replied, backing out of the alcove. "I've got no mind to be bothered by this. I'll be off to find some creamed ice. See you boys later."

"My name is Downy, last scion of the falcon cast, and this is my trophy, Trophy."

"Charlie," I corrected.

"We're here to speak with Monarch Mola," Downy said, glancing around to make sure Cheri had gone. "We seek an audience with the Phoenix. Will you let us in?"

"Well now, you've come to the right place," Red said, "This is the Royal Entrance to the Palace of the Kingdom of Town. We could let you in to see the Monarch."

"We could let you in," Black continued, "Except, as he said, this here is the Royal Entrance. If you're not royalty, we can't let you in. You'll have to use the other side, the Supplicant's Entrance."

"What are you talking about?" I asked. "How are we supposed to do that? Are we supposed to go around, or something? This door is carved in the side of the Ring! There's no other side!"

Red turned to Black. "Is he talking nonsense? I always said those Wingless had no sense. Everything has another side."

"Except, perhaps," Black noted, "A thought. But it has no sides at all, so having another side is out of the question."

Red nodded, rolling his eyes. "But," he said, "Even that is debatable, depending on your train of thought."

"That's always bothered me," Black said, "Why use a train to transport thoughts? It's so inefficient!"

"So, can you tell us how we might get inside to see His Majesty?" I snapped.

"Yes, we could," said Red.

"And how do we do that?" I asked.

"Oh, that? You can use this door here," Black said. "It's the one and only way to get inside."

"Sure is. We take protecting Monarch Mola very seriously," Red said. "Guarding this door is serious business."

"You just said this door was the Royal Entrance!"

"No, we said that *this* side of the door is for royalty," Black said, "The other side of the door is for supplicants. Listen carefully, please! We don't have all day to explain."

"What he's saying is: we could open it for you," Red said, "If you wanted to get to the other side. Is that what you were trying to say?"

"Yes! That's what I want!" I said. Downy shook his head, telling me it wasn't worth my energy. "Would you gentlemen please open the door, so we might pass through the portal and speak with His Majesty?"

"Sure, of course! Why didn't you say so in the first place? You could have been in the throne room right now," Red said. "I'm telling you now, it's like Wingless speak a different language altogether."

"I hear what you're saying," Black agreed, "But really, it's not their fault. They're missing their most important parts, after all. Let's get on with this then."

Trying to restrain my temper, I watched the guards tap on the obsidian portal with their weapons. The door split down the middle, each half receding into the wall beside it. Standing in the open threshold was a small bird about half Downy's size, colored black with yellow stripes on his face.

"Masters Downy and Trophy," he said, "My name is Ramsay. I will be your escort and translator through the Palace of the Kingdom of Town. Please follow me, if you will."

"I told you," Downy whispered as we walked into the dark tunnel, "These people up here are a little bit different."

We followed Ramsay for several minutes through a dark maze of tunnels. The whole time, he proclaimed the glories of the Kingdom of Town. He regaled us with stories of the days when the Kingdom was but a single hole in a cliff, before the mountain was turned into a molehill. The first wave of stonepeckers made it habitable, but the current royal family of Crow ousted them before they could get comfortable. I zoned out, pouring all of my focus into remaining upright, until we arrived at the throne room.

"Welcome to the Throne Room of the Palace of the Kingdom of Town," Ramsay cried, "All rise for Monarch Mola!"

At least twenty birds lined either side of the room, sitting with their wings crossed beneath their breasts. They stared at my entourage as we made our way to the center of the chamber. Our guide stopped some yards from the back of a stone throne nearly as tall as the ceiling.

The great stone throne before us rotated to reveal His Majesty's Royal Highness, one corpulent inch at a time. Sitting in the concrete seat was a humongously fat bird with a dark purple body. A shock of white feathers stood out on Mola's head, a powerful plume in the place of a crown. Extravagant tailfeathers of verdant green and violent violet streamed down from His Majesty's glutinous bottom, weaving odd upholstery for his throne. Mola opened his mouth to speak, but his beak was trapped by his chest's flabby girth. The only sound to escape was an unintelligible gurgle.

"Ghguurrlhhggruulgg," he intoned, looking at us with expectant eyes.

Downy and I fidgeted, unsure as to how we should respond.

"Ahem," Ramsay coughed, "His Majesty would like to welcome you, honorable falcon, to the Royal Court of the Kingdom of Town. Your noble caste precedes you. And you, young Wingless, His Majesty acknowledges your presence."

"Thanks," I nodded, adding as an afterthought, "Your Majesty?"

"Thuurmmugglglghhunumml," Monarch Mola continued.

"The King asks that you state your business and stop wasting his time already, he has so many other important things to do," Ramsay interpreted. "Also, Chef, he is now ready for his supper. Twice cracked corn, if you will."

An ashen bird with legs as long as its neck scuttled away in a cloud of feathers. "Always the twice cracked! Never a break!" it squawked into the distance.

"Well, Your Majesty," I started, unsure whether I should address the bloated Monarch or our translator. "We've come to visit the Phoenix. We must ask her advice on some very important issues. What must we do in order to earn an audience with her?"

Mola laughed. The simple vibrations of his diaphragm sent ripples up and down his monstrous breast. "Doohhoohhoohhunulhhruurgghunhunhu."

"His Majesty says he does not remember sending for a jester, but he is pleased that you are so naturally hilarious. It is a rare talent to make him chuckle so vigorously. He is now out of breath, but seriously, does the Wingless one truly think himself worthy of an audience with the Manifestation of

Beauty Herself? Is he capable of conversing with the Arbiter of All Knowable Knowledge? His Majesty thinks not."

"Now, King Mola," I started. "You must be reasonable. Don't look down on me just because I have no means to fly. I came a long way to see the Phoenix, and it's for a good cause. Tell him, Downy!"

Downy glared at me, his eyes accusing me of lunacy. "Of course, Your Majesty is wise and just. His wings could lift the Island itself to the stars. Please forgive my Trophy's insolence. He is not from around here; he knows not what he says. Maybe, just maybe, would His Honor consider giving the foreign Wingless a chance to earn the right to visit the Phoenix?"

Mola considered this proposition for several minutes, mulling it over like a lukewarm wine. When he reached his final decision, he began to laugh deep and slow. His belly heaved and sagged, threatening to topple his throne and crush his loyal subjects.

"He, he, he, he, mmununumppaarrgajajaja!"

The royal audience began to titter behind their wings, beaks tactfully hidden.

I was not amused. "What's so funny?"

Ramses spoke. "His Majesty has deigned to grant your request. He likes the Wingless boy's face. A surprising beauty comes from behind those lips. One week from tonight is the annual Kingdom Pageant. If the Wingless one competes and wins the

Pageant, His Majesty will grant both of you access to the Phoenix. If the Wingless one loses, neither of you will be allowed granted entry to make your queries and you shall both act as His Majesty's personal corn crackers for one Crow year."

I stomped my foot. The backwards ways of the mountain folk had long since irked me. "That's not fair! Surely Downy can earn his entry some other way."

"Meh," Mola said.

"The Monarch has spoken," Ramsay said. "Please excuse yourself. His Majesty would like you to remain out of his sight until the Pageant. He has too much stuff to do before then and does not wish your faces to disturb His dinner."

Two cardinal crows armed with quarterstaffs escorted us out of the throne room, terminating our encounter with the royal court. Once outside the Palace of the Kingdom of Town, Downy started ambling back toward the Azure Egress. "We might as well start back down now," he said, "If we get started right away, we can ditch that bitch Cheri and make it back to my family's clearing by nightfall tomorrow. I can have you good and stuffed by week's end."

"Wait, wait! Why are we leaving now? Don't you think we should at least try to win this competition? I mean, really, how difficult could it be to win a pageant?"

"Trophy! You've got no wings! You are fundamentally flawed in the realm of beauty. It's impossible for you to win. I don't have any desire to be the corn cracker for that buffoon."

"Now, why does that have to be the case? I think it's perfectly reasonable for me win. I'm not perfect, but I'm a little handsome. I'm at least a little bit cute, right? Anyway, there's sure to be a talent portion, too. Maybe I have some skill that I haven't realized yet. I can do this! It will be a triumph for Wingless everywhere."

"Poor, poor Trophy. You just don't see it. You've got no chance. The Monarch just wants you to dance around like a fool so his court can have a laugh. You won't be doing your kind any favors, just perpetuating stereotypes."

"Downy, I'm going to do this," I said, "There are no other options. You can leave if you must, but I'm going to stay and try my best. I'm too close to knowing some answers! I can't just quit now."

"Quit what now, sugar?" Cheri asked, appearing beside me licking a bowl of milky white liquid. "You know the old saying, quitters never perspire? It's not true. They're the worst of all. Creamed ice, either of you?"

"Can you believe this guy?" Downy squawked. "He's gotten himself entered in the Kingdom Pageant, thinking he can win the grand prize! Tell him he's crazy!"

Cheri gave Downy an empty gaze. "And why, don't you think he can win? You're such a wonderful companion, Master Downy. I'm surprised you don't have more friends. Tell me,

Charlie, why did you enter yourself in the Pageant, anyway?"

"Stubborn pride, I guess," I said. "I mean, I'm handsome, right?"

"Oh, Charlie, you're so pretty I want to dress you up like a princess and hold you for ransom! I'll tell you what. I've come to every Kingdom Pageant since I exited the Mists. I'm willing to help you prepare for this year's Pageant and make sure you're a winner, whatever your real reason is. Come on, I'll help you put together costumes and a performance piece. How does that sound?"

I nodded, ignoring Downy's pleading pout. "Teach me to sing!"

SUPPLEMENT

The next week was a long, terrible montage of trial-and-error through which I was never quite able to learn from my mistakes. Cheri attempted to teach me some basic dance moves, but I always confused my left and right feet. I tried my hands at acrobatics, but that effort ended with my hands tied. The lone pageant skill that I could perform with any semblance of ability was singing.

"You've got such a wonderful voice," Cheri said, "It's got such a nice timbre I'd love to cut out your vocal chords and use them to string my guitar."

"Well, thanks," I said, still unsure how to react to Cheri's brand of compliments.

"And, you're able to hit every note with surprising precision. But, sweetie, listen," she continued, "You've got to remember the lyrics. Otherwise, you've got no shot at the crown."

"I know," I whined, "Let me try again, I'm sure I'll get them right this time!"

I'd been trying to learn one song for almost three whole days. *A Fine Young Cannibal* was a traditional mountain shanty that had been written by a Wingless visitor years ago. I chose it as my performance piece because I hoped it might rouse some Wingless spirit. Three days later, I still didn't know what the damn verse was going on about.

Every time I practiced, the melody came out with perfect pitch, but the lyrics seemed to change. It wasn't that I forgot them; they wouldn't come out how they were supposed to sound. I could even have the written lyrics in front of me and I would screw them up. Every time I sang a verse, the words would slip off my tongue like lyrical custard, falling in a messy heap on the audience's ears. The chorus was worse, verbal vomit that had no rhyme or rhythm. No matter how many times I rehearsed, I would always fail in the exact same way.

Making everything worse was an endless barrage of nightmares. Every night, without fail, I would wake in the middle of the night screaming bloody murder. The same faceless stranger came back every night to haunt my dreams with an endless supply of tortuous devices. One night, I dangled upside down as he poured electric insects down my pants. The bugs shocked me and bit me until I woke up shouting. The next night, I was paralyzed on a cold, metal table. The stranger tapped my body all over with a strange wand, part of me disappearing with every touch. When, finally, my head disappeared, I cried myself awake. I was also drowned in gelatin, gobbled by a dozen Werefish, frozen and shattered, and shot from a cannon into the wall of the Ring. The worst nightmare, however, came on Pageant's eve.

I saw Vespa, surrounded by swirling Mist. I ran to greet her but my feet took me nowhere. She remained just out of reach no matter how fast I charged forward. I called out to her and she looked around, searching for the source my voice. She could hear me, but not see me running. As I kicked

144

at invisible ground, I saw the robed wanderer glide in and embrace Vespa from behind. She reached back and stroked his face, which remained just out of sight beneath his white hood, before turning to view him. Vespa returned the stranger's embrace, leaning in to kiss his obscured lips. As their encounter grew more passionate, razor tendrils of Mist began to dismantle my body, cutting me apart at each joint. I was left a pile of parts on the ground in the Mist realm while Vespa and the stranger flew away to unknown scenery. I woke with a yelp of frustration and wrath, nearly smacking Cheri with my flailing arms.

"Come now, sugar," she said, "It's all right. It was only a dream. They're all just dreams! Calm down, you've got a big day today."

The night of the Pageant had arrived, and I had no surefire plan for victory. Cheri was taking her time with my trappings, preparing me as calmly as a mother might bundle up her child before he went out to play in a snowstorm. I was grateful. Every minute she idled would save me a second of terrible embarrassment.

"You look so dreamy I want to mash you up and spread you on my toast. Take a look for yourself," she said.

I grabbed a vanity mirror from the table to gaze upon my transformed self. I fogged the glass with a gasp of surprise.

"My reflection!" I cried. "I can't see me! I'm not there!" I rubbed the space where my eyes should have been gazing back at me. I tilted and spun the frame, hoping that it was a trick of the light, nothing more. "What happened?" I moaned. "Where'd I go? Can you see me?"

I thrust the mirror as far from me as my arm would go, and turned my head away. It was painful to look at the void where I should have been.

"No, sugar," Cheri said, "I don't see you either. Is that so strange?"

"Of course it's strange," I freaked, "Don't you think it's a little odd, at least? I should be there! Shouldn't I?"

"Oh, I don't know," Cheri said, "I've certainly heard about some Winged that don't have reflections. But then, it's usually those that have done deals with the Warlock."

An idea snapped into alignment inside my head. "I did have a reflection, some time ago. I saw myself on the surface of river water. It's the one solid idea I have of what I look like, and it was quite choppy at best. But still, I know it was there! What did you mean when you said that the Warlock might have taken some other folk's reflections?"

"Well, child," she continued, "Certain people get greedy, looking for power or wealth or love. Whatever they are unsatisfied with, he tells them he can fix it. He offers them a trade. They get this power or that opportunity but lose their reflections or shadows or whatever Lucien wants."

"What could he possibly want with all those things?"

"I don't know, child!" Cheri protested. "I don't like to deal with those folks anymore. They're all perverts or narcissists or mass murderers or all of the above! I haven't talked to any other Were-beasts in years. That life, it's a part of my past. It happened, I was there, and I did horrible things to good people. I can accept that, but nothing says I have to embrace it any longer."

"I'm sorry," I said, "I didn't mean to assume anything. It's just, well, I've got reason to believe the Warlock took my reflection away without giving me anything in return."

"And why might he do something like that?"

I took a deep breath and mentally apologized to Downy. During the last week, I'd spent most of my time working with Cheri. I'd gotten to know her at least as well as I knew myself. Admittedly, that was not very well. Something in the manners of the buxom bird-lady struck me as honest. She was all too trustworthy, so I relayed to her every detail about my adventure.

"Well sure, sugar," she said, when I was finished. "He didn't give you nothing! He's given you an opportunity for power, as long as you abide by his contract's rules. Just reclaim all of your lost possessions and you'll get your reward. Your ultimate weapon or whatever."

"But I didn't sign any contract!" I whined.

"You didn't have to do anything, Lucien can accept the deal in your name. It's one of the Rules."

I collapsed forward. "Just once, I would like a to get good look at this rulebook."

"Wouldn't we all, child, wouldn't we all," she said, slapping me on the back. "Now straighten up, you can deal with that reflection tomorrow. Tonight, you've got yourself a Pageant to win."

Three hours and twenty-six songs about the Glories of the Monarch of the Kingdom of Town later, I was dripping with sweat and emitting anxious vapors. Standing in the wings of the theater, I watched all the other Pageant contestants strut their wares across the stage. Nervous tremors wracked my body, head to toe. The only sure cure for my anxiety was to just get it all over with and move on. I needed to go out onto the stage, finish my embarrassing rendition of a classic Mountain folksong, drown my sorrows in some raspberry cordial, and prepare for a year of corn-cracking. I had one more performance to endure.

The previous Pageant's top bird gave me a sassy look before making an entrance with flair of an equal attitude. She was a snowy owl, with short, soft feathers that reminded me of the sand where I'd washed up on the Island. I wished with every bone in my body to be back on the beach, comfortably numb. I watched the snow owl give an erotic dance, filled with sexy semi-gyrations of her hips and a climatic complete rotation of her head. She rode a wave of applause and cheers back behind the curtains, a smug smile on her beak. As my name, "Trophy Charlie," was called out onstage, she gave me a soul-crushing wink.

Shuddering under the pressure of imminent failure, I pranced to the center of the stage. The audience was huge. At least three hundred eager avians locked their eyes on my Wingless frame. At the back of the theater, Mola sat stuffing his face with barrels of birdseed. Spotlights descended and converged into one massive beam, scattering my vision into a kaleidoscope of lights and darks. I tried to sing, but the notes got stuck in my throat's arid labyrinth. A short squeaky cough emerged instead of music.

I closed my eyes, wincing in preparation for the boos that would follow my embarrassing start. At that moment, I wanted to be anywhere else. I would have been much happier back on the ocean floor than I was there, baring my weakness on stage. Deep in the dark Mists, lost to the Weres, a bigger grin would have crossed my face than the grimace I bore for the crowd. Worst of all, I couldn't even imagine the face I was making. All memories of my self-image had vanished. I was ready to give up my dreams of meeting the Phoenix and defeating Lucien, if only the embarrassment would stop.

Before I could surrender, a rogue epiphany appeared, zooming up through my inner vision, saving me from hell. I realized that I was no longer myself, having stepped out in front of the crowd. Somewhere, between the theater's wings and the center of the stage, I had stepped through a transmogrification device, a magical transformer that amplified the subtle vibrations of my soul. My old identity was unimportant, as if I had not existed before that very moment. On the stage I was exactly who I was supposed to be. Better yet, I could assume the role of whoever I wanted to become, making that identity as real as any. With this realization, lyrics came flowing from my lips as freely as though I'd already sung them ten thousand times:

A fine, young cannibal is a precious, pert thing,

Who knows the taste of her own skin.

She's been picked down to nothing; she is her own queen,

And knows exactly where she begins.

A Devil ate my insides, but it left this pretty shell.

My body ever hungers while my organs rot in Hell.

I wanted for to find a feast and overfill this hole,

Yet everything that I consumed refused me from my goal.

I tried a tasty tartlet, but she left me bittersweet.

I cooked a kooky cutter, but he took me in the street.

I fried a Frenchy friar, but he kept me from my pants.

I spread a lady marmalade, and lost my love of dance.

I ate an age-old Angel, but it only made me cross.

When I was out of options, then I thought that I had lost.

A fine, young cannibal is a wily, weird wight,

Which knows the taste of its own skin.

It's been wicked down to nothing; it is its own knight,

And knows exactly where it begins.

I took my foot and put it in; my mouth was open wide.

My knees and thighs did follow, though I choked up on my side.

I forced myself to swallow it, until I reached my chest,

And lost the sense of hollowness when I consumed the rest.

My head went down more easily than skeptics might suspect,

And I was gone completely, not a spec left to detect.

And in my state of nothingness, I found something of worth,

There were no holes for filling up or any dear old dearth.

A fine, young cannibal is a dashing, dear thing,

Who knows the taste of his own skin.

He's been dicked down to nothing; he is his own king,

And knows exactly where he begins.

I paused for a moment, allowing the last notes of my song echo through the audience's ears. There was not another sound, for I had not left any sonic space unfilled. Still, I could not help worrying about my performance. Just as panic was beginning to creep back up my toes, His monstrous Majesty clapped His wings. The thunder of His applause woke the rest of the crowd from their auditory coma and they began to cheer harder and harder. The din of their fervor elated my ego to unprecedented heights. The rest of the night was a blur, a riotous orgy of smiling faces, bright lights, and epic congratulations. I felt as though I was flying on invisible wings.

Just when I thought I couldn't get any higher, the universe sent me a glorious surprise.

"Hey, Charlie. I didn't realize you could sing so well," said a familiar voice. "Maybe we should start a band. You take lead vocals, I'll take the violin."

I turned to see the silky pink mop that I'd been missing for what seemed like an eternity. "Vespa! You're here!" I ran to her and knocked her off-balance with a zealous embrace a week in the making. "I can't believe it! I was beginning to think I might never see you again!"

"Whoa, I'm happy to see you too," she admitted, returning my hug with a more subtle intensity. "I'm glad I caught up to you. I wouldn't have missed that show for the world!"

"What are you doing here? What happened to your father? Why aren't you off in the valley, conquering our enemies?"

Vespa sighed. "Well, things got a bit complicated, once I left. My adventure started off fine and dandy. When I started exploring the Mists, it felt like I was some great pioneer. I even made a map, marking off the few landmarks I could make out. But, just when I thought I was making progress, the damn fog would spit me out at the base of the Azure Egress, right at the crack of dawn. Then the Mists would disappear, and I would have to wait until nightfall for them to return. I spent a whole week camped out there, Charlie! Seven nights I tried to navigate the Mists, with not a clue to show for it! So, I decided to give up on my silly notion and came back to find you. I just knew you would be more successful! I knew you could do it, Charlie! You can do anything!

"And now I'm here, begging your forgiveness. I need you, Charlie. I was wrong to be so selfish. Can you forgive me?"

I blushed. "Yeah, of course. I understand. You had to try doing things your own way. Now that I think about it, I had to do this for myself, too."

"I knew you would understand!" Vespa sighed and gave me a tighter hug. "So, do you think maybe we could ask the Phoenix about how to navigate the Mists? That's where Lucien took my father, I'm so sure of it! He said he wouldn't interfere with our progress, but here I am, unable to find my way to what he has stolen from me. If only we could get though the Mists!"

"Okay, okay," I said, "I'll use one of my questions to ask how we can do that. I've already figured out what I'm missing, anyway."

"What did Lucien take?"

"He took my reflection."

Vespa pursed her lips. "What would he want with that?"

"I've got no idea! It doesn't seem like it should have any value to anyone but me. And even then, it's only good for showing me what I look like. I didn't even know that when I washed up on the Island shore and I was just fine then. I certainly don't care what I look like, now."

"Well, sure, Charlie, but don't you like knowing how you are? How other people perceive you? Don't you enjoy figuring out all the little things that make up your identity?"

"I don't really think my face has very much to do with my identity. If anything, it confuses me. Just now, on stage, I created my own identity for the first time since I woke up nameless. It was surreal. For those brief moments of song and dance, I was exactly who I was supposed to be. I knew my true name, because it was one I gave myself. It has nothing to do with my reflection. If anything, that image was just getting in my way."

"Well, I'm sorry," Vespa sighed, "Don't you like being Charlie?"

I took her hand, squeezing it gently. "No, don't misunderstand me. I love being Charlie. That's definitely what I want to be called. But, finally, I know what Charlie is supposed to mean."

Vespa nodded. "I hear you. At least, I think I know what you're saying. Before, Charlie was just the word I named you. It was nothing more than gibberish syllables. Now, it's who you are."

"Bingo!" I nodded and smiled. "Hey, Vespa?"

"What's up, Charlie?"

"Don't run off on your own again, okay? Let's stick together from now on."

Vespa didn't say anything, but squeezed my hand tighter than a machinist's wrench. We talked for a long while after that, about little things of no importance, meaningless chatter. Or, it might have been the most meaningful conversation of all time, concerning the purpose of existence itself.

I don't really remember. As far as I cared, it was the most important conversation I could have: it was one I shared with her.

When I fell asleep that night, my face was covered by a smile bright enough to cut through any thickness of Mist and, for the first time in a week, no terrible nightmares haunted the umbrage of my slumber.

MORPHOLOGY

"Mmojorrommdohohobo," Mola mumbled into a large mug of coffee.

"His Majesty was moved to tears by your performance, Trophy Charlie the Wingless. He has never before imagined such beauty, nor did he expect it from an incomplete person. He would like to offer you honorary royalty status, but that would involve bypassing too many statutes for him to even bother. Instead, he hopes you will be satisfied if you and all your companions are granted audiences with the Phoenix. Excepting, of course, the filthy Were-woman."

"Yes!" Vespa, Downy, and I cried out together. Cheri stood watching us from the throne room's threshold, smiling her sultry smile, devouring yet another creamed ice.

"Psappogojajajalo," Mola gurgled, smiling. For once, I didn't need a translator to understand exactly what the Monarch meant to say.

Later that day, Red and Black and Ramsay escorted Vespa, Downy, and me further up the stairs of the Azure Egress. We ascended the stairs until they came to an abrupt end at another grand hole-in-the-wall. This hole, however, was in the side of the tallest mountain on the Island, the Azure Peak, the peak I had seen in my first moments of consciousness. If I had stood on top of the Ring up there, I could have pointed to the exact spot where I had washed ashore. My exhaustion made it feel like I had traveled much further than that.

"Please enter, Trophy and friends," Ramsay said, "The Phoenix has been waiting for you. The guards and I will be right here, so don't try anything funny." I took Downy's wing and Vespa's hand and led them inside the mountain. Some strong arms and sharp fists had carved out the entrails of the mountain, leaving a huge chamber inside where we encountered the Phoenix.

Gripping a plain wooden pole was the largest pair of wings I had ever seen. They were tremendous but flat, as though they had been cut from giant poster board. Radiant patterns shifted through the wings as they flapped. The exact shapes were impossible to define. Infinite permutations of gold and crimson and sienna swirled about like sand dunes in a windstorm. Behind the large mast, I saw the Phoenix's body, a slender, black cylinder. At the top of the Phoenix's stalky form waved two extravagant antennae, like fluffy, orange palm fronds. They waggled as we approached, alerting the grand creature to our presence.

My companions and I stood in awe as the chaos on the wings settled into a familiar shape. A smiling face appeared, stretched across the breadth of both wings, with eyes and mouth as dark as chocolate. The face mouthed words as the Phoenix spoke.

"Welcome, visitors. You made for an unforgettable evening last night. The mountainfolk will not forget your face for a long time, Trophy

Charlie. Thank you for bringing some joy and meaning to their dreary, monotonous lives. You have certainly earned an audience with my knowledge and me. Please, will you hasten your inquiry so that I may return to contemplating the infinite?"

I turned to my companions. "Well, who wants to go first?"

"The pink-haired pixie should go first," the Phoenix boomed. "That's a free answer. You made that query before I had gotten myself settled, so I won't hold it against your question stock."

Startled, Vespa stepped out before the Phoenix, her tiny frame dwarfed by the gigantic Winged insect. "Hmm, great Phoenix, where will I find my father? I mean, oh shit, that's going to count against me, isn't-" she cut herself short of wasting another query, "Yes, it is."

"This was a wasted question. You already knew the answer, but it's nice to be sure of your convictions, isn't it? The Warlock currently holds your father captive in his fortress, deep within the Mists. Please, ask your second query."

Vespa gathered her thoughts to ask a more productive question. "How can we navigate the Mists to find my father?"

"The select few who may successfully travel through the Mists are those who have already traveled through them. You must find one who has this ability."

"So, what is that supposed to mean? I can't travel through the Mists because I've never traveled through the Mists? That's stupid. How does anyone ever get through the Mists the first time? Hmm. What about that?"

"It's just the way things are. One of many rules you will discover throughout your life. I didn't make it up. Also, you have no more questions. Next up, the curious falcon. Ask me what you wish to know."

I put my arm around Vespa, who was beginning to panic. "Don't worry," I said, "We've got lots of questions left. We'll figure this out. We just need to figure out the Phoenix's rules. We'll have Downy clarify what the Phoenix meant."

Downy stepped forward, ready to do his part and ask his queries. "Where can I find my missing hunter's abilities?"

"You will find your missing skills in the Ides Marsh, if you search high and low. But, you must seek with care. You might not recognize your skills in their new form."

"Perfect. That's great," Downy squawked. "That's all I needed to hear. Can I give my extra question to Trophy?"

"No, not anymore. Perhaps if you had been more careful with your phrasing, I would have let you. But, no. I gave you fair warning and you did not prepare yourself. Too bad."

"Downy," Vespa hissed through her teeth, "You screwed us over! Come here, I'm going to sock you in the beak, you tit."

Downy put his beak in the air. "My prize, I am no such dumb bird. I was only trying to help our situation."

"Calm down," I said, "We need to focus. I have two more questions, I'll make them count for all I can manage."

The Phoenix was growing ever more impatient. "Please ask your first query, Wingless one. I have but a few trillennia to mull the universe before the river of time itself runs dry."

I paused for a moment, trying to phrase my question as intently as possible. "Phoenix, what must I do to reacquire the reflection that has been taken from me?"

"Ah, excellent, Wingless one. You have learned from the mistakes of your companions. Your cleverness belies your lack of beauty. Goodness. Why you would want to regain such an ugly reflection is beyond even my vast pool of knowledge. Nevertheless, I shall answer your question to the best of my abilities.

"In truth, you already have the object that you seek in your possession, but you do not know its form. When you recognize its shape, you must grab it tight and hold it close, no matter how it might protest. Embrace it until it acknowledges its place in your mirror. Ask your second query, Wingless one."

I sputtered, choking back my urge to waste a question on divining more about the Phoenix's murky riddle. There was a purpose hidden behind each of the Goddess's words, obscured by the stress of my current situation. I would have to ponder her phrasing after I asked my other important question.

Vespa was waiting for a more definite answer to her original question. I had the opportunity to fix her mistake; I could have asked, "What must we do to meet the one who will take us through the Mists to Vespa's father?" Yet, something else was bothering me, a nagging suspicion that forced all other queries off the tip of my tongue.

"Why is it that the Islanders place so much emphasis on the beauty of wings?"

The face on the Phoenix's wings shifted to a sharp frown. "Isn't it obvious? I am the Manifestation of Ultimate Beauty and almost all of my form is Winged. Therefore, the further you stray from my shape, the less beautiful you are, silly Wingless."

"But, Phoenix, I know your true form," I said, a stream of knowledge seeping into my brain. "You are also the Goddess of Rebirth, are you not? You burn away only to be born again, creating a new identity out of your previous form's ashes. Tell me, Phoenix, was your previous identity Winged?"

The Phoenix was beyond irate. Her wings sparkled and whirled until they burned crimson. "You have already wasted all of your queries. I owe you no more answers! Guards!"

"It's all right," I continued, sopping up the soggy facts as they spilled all over my brain. "You don't need to tell me anything. I already know the truth. There's no doubt in my mind. Try and deny it. You can't lie! You're the Phoenix! At least, you are now. I'm sure you were once a Wingless, like me. Tell me how to change! I want to be reborn like you! I can do it!"

"Guards! Guards!" the Phoenix bellowed, frightened by my divination. "Take these visitors away! They have long since overstayed their welcome!"

Red and Black shambled inside, weapons leveled, and gestured that we should take a hint and step outside. After sharing a brief glance with my companions, we acquiesced. As we exited, I heard the Phoenix whisper a terse goodbye for my ears alone.

"Farewell, clever Trophy Charlie. Know this: anybody can grow wings, as long as she is willing to first burn herself away."

"What was that all about, Charlie?" Vespa asked, once we had been ushered away from the Phoenix's lair. "How did you know just the right things to say to piss off that old bird?"

"Yes, excellent job at making us unwelcome everywhere on the Island in less than five minutes," Downy quipped.

I shook my head. "I don't know. It came to me out of nowhere. A memory from long ago, maybe. It was strange. When I was a child, I think I knew another, smaller Phoenix. It was more common, certainly less knowledgeable, but still the same species, at least. The thing is, it wasn't born that way. It was a tiny wingless worm at first, bound to the earth and ugly as sin. One day it died and hardened into a nasty corpse. Then, some days later, it reanimated in the form of the Phoenix we just met. At least, that's what I thought of the process as a kid. I don't know why I remembered that right then."

"Really! Of all the memories to suddenly remember, you had to get one that would interfere with our chances of navigating the Mists and getting my father back. I mean, couldn't you have waited to piss off the Arbiter of All Knowable Knowledge until after you asked her to clarify my answer?"

"Oh, hush," I said, "I've got a plan."

We found Cheri waiting for us outside the Palace of the Kingdom of Town, preparing three bowls of creamed ice for us. "How was your meeting with the Phoenix, kids? Need some treats to wash down that wisdom?"

"It was disastrous!" Downy shouted. "It's unlikely that we'll be allowed back into the Phoenix's chamber for the next hundred millennia or so."

"Oh, shut up, bird," I said, "Cheri, I need to ask you an important favor."

"Shoot, child. I'll do anything for my favorite Wingless diva."

"I need you to take us through the Mists to find Vespa's father. The Phoenix said the only way through the Mists is to have someone who's been through it before. I don't know who else to ask."

"Oh, I'm sorry, but there's no way I can do that, sugar," Vespa frowned, her limpid eyes shining dark. "I've been removed much too long. I don't know my way around there anymore. It's surely changed beyond my abilities. I'm really sorry. I lost touch with that part of myself too many years ago."

"Well, shit," I said, earning a half-hearted smile from Vespa, "What are we supposed to do now? We don't know all that many Were-beasts that aren't intent on devouring our souls."

"Come now, honey, I wouldn't give up hope just yet," Cheri nudged me. "I'm not the only Were who has left the Mists over the last few years. I know there were a few others who agreed with my ideals. More specifically, they disagreed with the way things were being run by the man in charge. There's sure to be one or two skipping about that might be willing to help our cause."

Downy narrowed his eyes, gazing down his long beak. "Didn't you say you stopped communicating with those types of people? Isn't that your excuse for being unable to stop the slaughter of my family?"

"Calm down," Cheri said, "I wasn't lying when I told you the truth. I haven't heard from any others since I been out. I have, however, heard of them. You have too, I'm sure. It's difficult to avoid the news. Thunderpuss has been seen-"

"No!" Downey quacked. "No way are we going to ask him for help. That can only end in disaster!"

I shrugged. "We don't have many options at this point. We might just have to settle for whatever help we can garner. Besides, what could be so terrible about this Thunderpuss?"

"Thunderpuss was one of Lucien's top lieutenants," Cheri explained, "He was a ruthless murderer, devouring many innocent birds on the Island. Also, well, let's just say that while Downy has no reason to hate me, he has plenty of reasons to hate Thunderpuss. Isn't that right, sweetie?"

Downy scowled in response. His hatred for this particular Were-beast was much too personal. I hoped he would be able to handle his rage, for the sake of our quest. We had no other options but to find this monster.

"Anyway," Cheri continued, "Thunderpuss left the Mists shortly after that tragedy. I'm not sure about the exact reason why it happened, but he and Lucien had some sort of falling out. The rift in their friendship was irreparable, so Thunderpuss went into exile. Now, he whomps around the Ides Marsh, chasing away any and everyone who comes too near."

"The Ides March! That's perfect! Downy, we can track down your missing skills while we try to meet this terrible beast!"

Downy maintained his armored silence, nodding slowly.

"Okay, it sounds like this fellow is our best lead toward getting through the Mists," Vespa said, raising one finger. "But, is there any reason why he won' t just chase us away, too?"

"No, child," Cheri continued, smiling, "He'll definitely come after us. I hope you can talk really, really fast."

MACROBIOLOGY

The next morning, Downy, Vespa, Cheri, and I left the Kingdom of Town behind us, embarking toward the Ides Marsh with our guides, Red and Black. As we descended the Azure Egress, a brisk wind picked up and inspired them to start singing.

"I do enjoy a good trudge through the sludge," Red sang.

"But, I heard that you also like budgies with pudge!" Black responded.

"I also like fudge, that you mustn't forget!"

"Don't you fret my dear friend, I like trumpet quartets."

"But don't you have a pet? Won't that poor birdie fret?"

"Though my baby will sweat, I can do as I please."

"You will listen with ease from your house in the trees."

"We'll catch some tunes on the breeze, 'til the sun disappears."

"With a couple of beers, we'll escape all our fears."

"Hear, hear! Here we go, it's the end of the verse."

"Though the next one is worse. Oh, Please don't be averse!"

Our guides maintained their tedious discourse for all three eventless days of our journey to the Ides Marsh. They never stopped for breath until we reached our final destination. However, by then the damage was done.

"So, this is the Ides Marsh," I said, "That long hike was too harsh."

"Oh, no, please don't you start," Vespa said, "Or I'll punch out your lights."

"Shh, be quiet you mites," Downy hissed, "There's no time for your fights."

"Now the evening's still light," Cheri muttered, "And our future is bright. So please focus your sights on our imminent goal."

"But we're in a deep hole and we've anted our souls," I cried.

Vespa raised her fist and shook it. "You'd better bolt before I lose control. Oh shit! What was that?"

A trumpeting moan ambled out of the swampy darkness, followed by a sonic web of guttural creaks. The silence after the noise was suffocating, the effect amplified by a subtle hint of *Eau de Necrosis* in the air.

"Well, this is as far as we're going to come," said Black, "And the moment is coming when we must go. Farewell!"

"You weren't half-bad," Red said, "For folk only half-good. So long!"

Without a trace, the guards vanished. Our party was stranded in the antechamber to a stagnant, rotting fen.

I laughed, trying to shake out my nerves. "Well, I don't suppose anyone was paying attention to how we got here?"

"No, I was much too busy focusing on ignoring those rakes!" Downy muttered.

Vespa nudged me in the arm and made a sweeping gesture toward the edge of the marsh. "After you, my liege!"

The four of us crept into the murky, knee-deep wetness. Cheri carried Downy up above the surface, so he wouldn't fall below and drown. Downy wriggled non-stop, trying to remain as uncomfortable as possible in his mother's arms. The water, if it could be called that, was colored an opaque shade of puke. Any treacherous drops in the bottom were obscured by thick swirls of sludge. We formed a line, with just a few paces between us. I led us as well as I could, though I had no idea where we needed to go, or what we would do when we got there. Cheri had been less than forthcoming with details on the Thunderpuss' appearance or temperament. Downy refused to speak on the subject.

"Can you at least tell me what I should be looking for?" I asked, swatting at a few rogue gnats. We'd been wandering for hours, sweltering under the sun's rays and the bog's sweat. There was little shade. The sole flora growing in the marsh were small patches of reeds scattered about "As far as I know, I'm dooming us to stinky death in this horrible bog."

"For peat's sake," Cheri said, "I can't help you. It's been years since I last saw the Thunderpuss. I can't even begin to place his face."

"Well, tell me something to keep me from going crazy. You said he was one of the Warlock's top generals, right? How did he earn such a prestigious position?"

"Well, to be honest, I heard a good many rumors about that. You know, some folks said that he was the Warlock's son. Others said that the Warlock only gave Thunderpuss rank because he was afraid of his raw power. Stranger still, some claimed they were lovers and the reason Thunderpuss left the Mists was over a simple lover's quarrel. Personally, I think all of those stories are too simple. It's got to be something real crazy!"

"But, what does he look like?" I asked. "You know all these rumors without knowing what he looks like?"

"I'm sorry, sugar, that's just how it goes sometimes when you live in a land of thick Mist."

"Um, it wouldn't happen to maybe look anything like that, would it?" Vespa asked, pointing at a mound of sludge that had begun to move.

With a sucking noise not unlike flesh being ripped from bone, a massive body unstuck itself from swampy goop a few yards to our right. The Thunderpuss stood, on four legs, twice as tall as Cheri, the tallest of our group. A thick golden fur covered his beastly body, dripping with marsh water. His forearms were an exception; they grew hairless, with a shape as human as my own. Thunderpuss slapped the water with his gigantic, pancake tail, indicating that the time had come to get serious. He opened his large duckbill in a terrible snarl. It looked rather out of place in the center of his furry face. It was a face that would have been cute but for the empty Were-eyes. Thunderpuss released a mighty bellow, rippling the surface of the marsh and stunning us with his epic stench. The noxious vapors implied that this Were-beast survived on a daily regiment of dirt, peat moss, and bacteria, with a little bit of raw murder on the side.

The mighty Thunderpuss charged through our chain, snapping us into two parties. Vespa and I fell forward and turned our momentum into a sprint. A quick glance over my shoulder showed me two good things: Cheri had kept hold of Downy and they were making a rapid escape in the opposite direction. Meanwhile, Thunderpuss was making a very slow turn in the thick marsh-water.

"Come on!" I encouraged, "Vespa, he's slow to turn! If we can just stay out of his path-"

Another roar flew from mighty lungs. Thunderpuss had regained his bearings and was rampaging toward our position. Monstrous splashes approached us faster and faster from the rear.

"Vespa, don't look," I cried. "Jump away from me when I say! Run as fast as you can away from me! We've got to split up."

Vespa glanced at me with wide eyes. "Charlie, no! We're supposed to stick together! I've learned my lesson! We shouldn't part!"

"Please! Trust me! On three! One! Two!"

"Charlie," Vespa rasped, "I want-"

"Three!" I yelled, cutting her off. "Go!"

We broke and I ran as fast as my body could cut through the thick water. I felt the hot air of Thunderpuss rushing past, in the direction I had been traveling just a second before. I smelt the blight of his wake. I couldn't stop to look back, knowing full well that every second I focused was another chance to survive. Breathing hard, the swamp air coated my lungs in its moist embrace. I would never take fresh air for granted, ever again.

I heard splashing mere feet behind me and my heart leapt up my esophagus, but the splashes sounded too small to be monstrous in origin.

"Vespa!" I coughed, "You were supposed to go in the opposite direction. The Thunderpuss was going to follow me and you'd be safe!"

"Oh yeah? How do you know he wasn't going to follow me? Besides, we're not supposed to separate, remember? You said it yourself, 'let's stick together from now on.' Can't you mean what you say, or at least say what you mean?"

"Later!" I yelled, hearing an attack bellow from Thunderpuss. "Get ready to dodge again! He's coming!"

But, the splashes of his dashes grew less intense. He wasn't coming after us, this time.

"Over here, you incomplete water-rat! Your mother ate underage earthworms, for the filthy pleasure of it all!" Downy shouted. "I've seen rocks run faster than you, you flaccid boob."

I couldn't fathom what he was doing, but I thanked him. Thunderpuss thrashed and grunted as he plummeted toward my avian companion, forgetting about our escape.

"This way!" Vespa dragged me by my arm into a thick thatch of reeds. Once inside, we paused, forgetting even to breathe, and watched turmoil unfold on the marsh.

"I say," Downy taunted, invisibly. "I've seen planes crash with more grace than you, big fella. You're much too dull to catch me. How about we play Hide-and-Go-Screw-Yourself? I'm over here!"

Thunderpuss jumped around, swatting at the places he thought Downy might be hiding. The Were-beast splashed wildly, displacing much marsh with his human arms.

"What is he doing?" I wondered aloud.

"Well, I'm just projecting my voice all over the marsh," Downy said, from right behind us. Vespa and I both jumped, almost falling out of our cover.

"Downy!" I cried. "I'm so glad you're all right! But, how the hell are you right here? I heard you way out there on the marsh?"

"I told you, I just did some projection, distracting Thunderpuss so you could escape. It was a traditional family skill, used in some of our more fanciful productions. I'd forgotten I could do it. Cheri provided me with the insults," Downy said, blushing.

Cheri waved from behind Downy. "You dropped this, back there," she said, handing Vespa her luggage.

"Thank you, Cheri. Hold on a minute," Vespa said, "Downy, you mean you can just cast your voice anywhere you choose?"

"No, I can project it. I can't cast it. I couldn't possibly do that, not since I lost my hunter's skills," Downy protested. "But, possibly, I might have accidentally made you think I did."

"No, you just did it! Deal with it!" Vespa said, a mite too loud. The bog foliage rustled tantalizingly. I prayed Thunderpuss would stay distracted, but an impatient roar reminded us that our battle was not yet over. The Were-beast was searching for any sign of our presence, ready to unleash his lycanthropic fury.

"How are we supposed to calm him down?" I whimpered. "He's a monster! He's going to kill us all! There's no way he'll talk to us, much less help us navigate the Mists."

"Now, sugar," Cheri said, "I've always said, it's music that calms the savage beast. You know? A pretty tune might lull him into a more tranquil state."

"So, what?" I replied. "Are we supposed to sing him a lullaby? I could maybe sing a song, but I have no idea what to do right now. Any suggestions would be more than welcome."

"Calm down, Charlie," Vespa said. "I've got it under control. While I was camped out, waiting for the Mists to come around, I spent a fair bit of time learning to play that instrument the old flamingo gave us. I got pretty good, it's real easy. We'll play something together, that should to the trick, I hope."

She opened her father's luggage and scrabbled through some junk before pulling out the instrument. It was a long squeezebox, with piano keys on one end. She pulled it apart and it pressed it together. It released a noise similar to chalk on a chalkboard, but with a subtle coat of harmony taking the edge off the cacophonous sound.

"What is that?" I asked, confusion amplifying my voice to near dangerous levels.

"It's the accordion, silly. Remember? The flamingo at Helmsdotter gave it to us in the hopes that it might help us defeat the Were-beasts. And,

175

look at us, we're about to use it for just that purpose!"

"But that's not the instrument he gave us! He gave us that stringed fiddle, the violin."

"Obviously not, Charlie. I'm holding the accordion right here. There was no violin. Check the luggage, if you want."

I scoured the contents of the suitcase. "I guess you're right," I admitted. "That's the only instrument I see, but I swear it was different before."

A frown wrinkled Vespa's face. "I'm beginning to worry, Charlie. All those times you had me convinced my memory was going bad... Well, maybe it's your memory we should be worried about, not mine."

I couldn't refute her logic. If I was wrong about this trivial fact, I couldn't be sure any of my other, important memories were legitimate. I still couldn't fathom how I had realized the truth of the Phoenix's origin. I swallowed a bit of saliva laced with doubt. There was no way I could be sure of anything anymore, aside from what was happening right before my eyes. Even those, I was beginning to doubt.

"Maybe you're right," I admitted, "But now is not the time to figure it out. We've got to calm this beast, or we won't survive the day. That is something we can all be sure about."

"Agreed," said Downy, "And I have a plan, if you two lovebirds would stop bickering. I need you to help me. I'm not going to be able to distract him with my projection, or casting, if you must. Trophy, I want you and Vespa to play a song and distract him while Cheri and I work a little magic. He'll probably charge right at you, and you mustn't move from you position. Do you trust me?"

Vespa nodded at me, but her eyes told me she was unsure.

"Will you at least tell us what you're about to do?" I asked. It was too late, Downy and Cheri had ducked under the marsh surface and disappeared. I looked out of the reeds, but couldn't even see a trace of ripples on the surface.

"Looks like we don't have many options," Vespa muttered. "Let's trust that turdly bird."

"Well, we could just run away," I said. "And come back with some sort of army?"

Vespa raised one eyebrow. "Oh yeah? Which army? Don't be such a wuss!"

Creeping out of the reeds, Vespa and I took up positions a few yards apart. There were no obstacles and no cover. Once Thunderpuss noticed us, there would be no stopping him from trampling us into the marsh and doing with our bodies whatever Thunderpuss liked to do.

"Are you ready?" I asked. "This could be the last thing we ever do together. We should pick a really good song."

"I was thinking A Fine Young Cannibal might be appropriate," Vespa replied, "Considering our inevitable fates."

I smiled, but couldn't quite laugh. "That'd be swell."

"Hey, Charlie, I really do- oh never mind," Vespa said. "Let's just do this. We can emote once we get out of here."

She picked up her squeezebox and pulled it taut. A single compression released a beautiful cacophony, ringing through the air and cutting a swathe through the bog's musk. I heard her chords and began to sing, though I could have refrained. It was another spell that compelled me to make melody for her, but I didn't mind. I was getting used to her powers over me.

I watched Thunderpuss charge at us. His eyes had transformed into spheres of pure death, focused on the termination of our mortal existence. Watching my demise rush towards me, I realized there were many worse ways to die. At least here, I'd chosen the time of my expiration. And I was doing something I loved with a person I liked very, very, very much. Yes, there were much worse ways to go.

I rapidly traveled through denial and anger and skipped over bargaining and depression altogether. As I gave myself over to immutable fate, I saw a shining ray of hope cast down from the heavens. Cheri appeared, charging at Thunderpuss from the side. She launched a brown cannonball at the beast. Downy glided onto Thunderpuss' spine.

With a glamorous twirl, he stabbed the Were in the back of the neck. Thunderpuss raked his fingers at Downy, trying to scrape the falcon off, but Downy held tight to the embedded machete. Thunderpuss tripped on his own feet and momentum carried him forward. His monstrous body skidded to a slimy halt. A few spasms later, the beast lay still.

Downy stood on its back, wings back, chest puffed as large as it might inflate. He was the very model of a regal hunter, posing for an eternal moment of glory over the prey he had never dreamed of catching.

MONOLOGY

"Downy, you're insane!" I hollered, "You did it! You saved us from an untimely trampling!"

"What was that all about?" gasped Vespa. "Why didn't you do any of that knavery ten minutes ago?"

"I don't know what happened," Downy admitted. He removed his weapon and slid down the side of his fallen quarry. "I just saw you, my precious trophies, in trouble. I knew I had to do something to save you and that idea popped into my head. I must admit, I'm not sure where it came from, or why I risked my life to save you. It's so unlike me."

"Oh, hush, darling," Cheri said, scooping Downy into her arms. "That was a wonderful thing you just did, nobody else could have done it half as well as you. You're a brave little falcon, just like your father. The nobility's in your blood." Instead of wriggling away, Downy was content to blush.

"Well now, isn't that just adorable?" a stale voice asked. Lounging in the air several yards above us, Lucien rest his chin on one hand. "The falcon found his hunter's skills at just the right moment. He recognized them and stole them back just as his friends were in danger! Oh, it's just so precious I can't even believe it!"

"You soulless maniac!" Downy yelled, shaking his wing at the sky. He squirmed out of Cheri's arms, landing with a splash, and slogged as close as he could get to his nemesis. "We're coming to slay you, Warlock, soon enough! I'll play croquet with your nasty face."

"We've taken back one of the things you stole from us, Lucien," I said. "And we've figured out what else you took. I know the Rules of your game, a little better now. At least, I know you're bound by your words. As soon as we find the other two items, you must give us the weapon we'll use to destroy you!"

"Oh, ho! That's the spirit!" Lucien said, clapping. "That's the feistiness I was hoping I'd hear from you. I was a little bit worried that you'd given up on defeating little old me."

"Yeah, like that'd ever happen," Vespa shouted, "You've got my mom on lock down, using them for your personal perversions! You're the worst person ever, man. Even your own kind doesn't like you!"

"Ah, yes, I see you've become acquainted with a few of my old friends," Lucien sighed. "It's such a sad thing to see people who were once so close to you become so distant. Time is a bad friend to everyone, mixing up thoughts and motives. It turns hearts around because they can't move forward, but they have to keep moving."

"I hope you aren't expecting any sympathy from me, you bastard," Cheri snapped. "Our friend ship sank long ago. I never agreed with your ideals to begin with, but then you had to go and kill my lover! You were always jealous of the men and women I chose for mates, but that time your actions were inexcusable. I'm helping these young Wingless get their vengeance on you, Lucien. Charlie is more of a man than you could ever hope to be."

"Is that so?" asked Lucien, tapping his lower lip. "That may be, or it may be not. I'm sure we'll find out, soon enough, assuming that you are able to find your way to my fortress. Considering that you just killed your best shot at getting through the Mists, I don't know how sure that future is."

"We'll find a way, you fiend," Cheri said, "Count on it."

"Yes, yes, I always could count on you, mon Cheri. I'm sure you'll do just fine," Lucien mumbled. "But I'm not just here to offer witticisms and compliments. I had a more specific agenda with a most particular human.

"Charlie, I've been watching your progress. You've been unusually resourceful. I was very impressed by how easily you rattled the Phoenix. I can't remember a time when she's ever been so scared. It makes me even more curious what you're capable of doing to this Island, even if we must conflict from time to time. So, I'm going to give you a present, free of charge."

"Yeah, right," I said, "Nothing is ever a gift, when it comes from you."

"No, really, this one is completely gratis," he refuted, "Think of it as a reward, for completing the first part of my quest, a taste of what you'll gain when you complete all three parts." He reached into his pants' pocket and pulled out a monochromatic, golden-brown rumbly, quite ordinary compared to all the others I'd seen. "Save it for a rainy day, when you're famished and desperate."

I caught the fruit, almost fumbling it into the slimy water. "Thanks, I guess. And what, pray tell, is it going to do to me? Expand my ears? Give me super-strength? Or will it just kill me straight away so that you don't have to dirty your hands?"

"None of those things, silly boy," Lucien said, grinning. "It's just incredibly delicious. That one is my favorite familiar. I have a feeling you'll find the taste unusually familiar."

I was tempted to throw the rumbly at Lucien's predator face, but I knew that he would just dodge it. He wouldn't do something like this without good reason. I couldn't afford to act before I knew what he was plotting. "If you like it, I can't imagine it being something that I'll enjoy. I'll put it away until I have something to wash the flavor out of my mouth."

"Very well, suit yourself," Lucien said. His body began to fade into the sky, now igniting with the setting sunlight. "Alas, I must excuse myself, beautiful people. I've got to get back to work. I've got some new projects that I need to manage and tidy up a bit. Ah, projects, projects, projects! Always getting in the way of my social life! Last night, one of my agents told me about this great pyramid on a lake, full of delicious souls. It's surrounded by water, but someone left a backdoor open."

"Helmsdotter!" I shouted. "No, you can't go there. It's a safe zone! The Mist can't cross water, it's in the Rules."

Lucien had been reduced to nothing more than a floating head. "There's a loophole in every Rule, Charlie. That's something you should probably always keep in the back of your mind. It's a very good Rule to live by, though I suppose there's a loophole hidden there, too. Loopholes within loopholes! Hmm, it just makes so much more sense to follow the Rules as written, doesn't it? To blindly follow the machinations of some greater order? Or, Charlie, are you the type of person who lives to break Rules? Give me your answer next we meet! I'm dying to know what you think. Bye for now!"

Lucien's head vanished except his eyes, petrified events horizon, which lingered around just long enough to watch us squirming with rage. A half-moment later, they blinked themselves out of existence.

"The nerve of that man-beast," Cheri muttered. "I can hardly contain myself!"

"He just appears whenever he likes, taunts us, and leaves us with riddles that don't make sense!" I crossed my arms. "Even if he wasn't trying to commit genocide, I'd want to kill him for being an annoying prick."

"Yes, you're all right, he's terrible," Vespa said, "But he makes a very good point."

"You can't actually agree with him on anything, can you?"

"Well, not exactly, "Vespa replied," But we did just kill off our best chance at getting through the Mists in one piece

"Oh, you didn't kill anything," a deep basso rumbled over the quagmire, "Just a sad, lonely Thunderpuss who was minding his own business until these meddling kids showed up." Thunderpuss rested his head on one of his human hands, not unlike Lucien had done in the air. "Now, what'd you have to go and do that for?" Thunderpuss moaned. His voice boomed like a detuned timpani banged by a rhythmless bard. "I've got a splitting headache and a knot in my back, thank you very little."

"I'm sorry?" I asked, sarcasm thinly veiled by my pitch. "You were the one trying to gobble us up! We were trying to defend ourselves!"

"You're lucky I didn't chop your head off, you loathsome cur!" Downy said, slashing his machete.

"Oh, no, no, no, no," Thunderpuss replied, "We were only playing Hide-and-Seek, weren't we? You all seemed so involved in the game, running amok like wild turkey buzzards. I thought we were having a good time together!"

"No, that was us trying to avoid being trampled to death," Vespa muttered. "Really? Don't you think you might have said hello or something, before roaring and charging at us?"

Thunderpuss paused and thought about this prospect. "Well, I suppose I might have, but then I would have lost the element of surprise! It would have become a whole lot harder for me to chase you down if I'd lost that."

"Yes, but then we might have played the game with you, instead of trying to kill you."

"Hum, that is a good point," admitted Thunderpuss. "I suppose that might also explain why everyone else who comes by runs away as soon as I try to play with them. Gosh, loneliness is such a vicious cycle. There's never anyone around to help you realize why you've become so lonely, which only makes you lonelier and harder to be around." The sad Were-beast dropped to his belly and began to blow bubbles under the bog surface.

"Don't get depressed, sugar, everyone makes mistakes," Cheri said, "I'm sure these fine folks understand it was just a miscommunication. You're so much fun I want to nearly-kill you all over again!" She nudged me sharply, nodding at the melancholy Were-beast.

"Of course, that's exactly what I was about to say," I mumbled, "Thunderpuss, we only came to the Ides Marsh because we hoped to meet your acquaintance! And to have fun!"

The bubbles stopped. Thunderpuss looked at me, waiting for a more believable explanation.

"We heard that you are a really great person! Very outgoing and, well, everyone says you're exciting, at the very least. And we were hoping that you might be willing to help us navigate the Mists."

"Oh, here it comes," Thunderpuss pouted.

"Well, see, we're looking for some things that were stolen from us. One is her father," I gestured to Vespa, "and the other is my reflection. We have good reason to believe that Lucien has taken them somewhere in the realm of the Mists."

"Ha! You're in a quarrel with Lucien? How preposterously ridiculous. You're no different than that horrible Warlock. You just want to use me for my abilities, but you don't actually want to be my friend. Pah! I wish I had crushed you all during Hide-and-Seek. If I didn't have such awful neck aches, I'd do it right now. Get out of my swamp, you mean-hearted jerks."

"Hush, hush, sweet Thunderpuss," Cheri said, stroking the side of the Were's mammoth skull. "We came looking to ask you for help, but that doesn't mean we don't want to be your friend. Lucien hurt you, didn't he? What happened between you two, anyway? You used to be so close."

Thunderpuss inched away from Cheri's soft touch. "You don't honestly want to hear my story; you're just trying to convince me to take you through the Mists. Just stop. Stop it before you embarrass yourselves."

"Look, you damn pity-hound, it's taking all of my will not to kill you again, for real this time," Downy shouted. "You did terrible things to my kin and I won't forget it, but we desperately need your help. Trust me, if there were any other way, we would have tried it. But, you're our only option for now. If that means you need to tell your sob story to some sensitive ears, then just do it already and quit begging for attention. Today will end either with you taking us where we want to go or us leaving you dead in the Marsh. The choice is yours."

"Well, maybe I'd rather die!" said Thunderpuss. He held his chin high, but his eyes remained cast low.

"He's not lying, you know," I said, "He can kill you, straight away. I can't do anything to stop him, that's for sure. If you help us, we can save the lives of innocent Helmsdotterians. Then maybe, just maybe, Downy's burning desire to finish you off and see your lifeless body float away will ebb enough so that he can tolerate your presence and not go through with it"

"Not likely," Downy muttered.

Thunderpuss sighed, his breath as rancid as a jar of mayonnaise lined with rotten bacon. "All right, all right. You convinced me, I'll tell you my woes! Lucien and I had always been such good friends. For as long as I can remember, we were best buddies, pals without limits! Before the Mists got snared by the Island, we were inseparable partners!"

"Wait, the Mists existed before they were on the Island?" I asked. "How could that be, I thought they were trapped here?"

"Well, yes, they're trapped here now, but that's because they're subject to the rules of the Island," Thunderpuss corrected. "But, long ago, the Mists could go anywhere. And we did! Lucien and I led our people all over the world! We caused ruckuses beyond your wildest imaginings, siphoning souls like they were going out of season! Seaside parties, rambunctious game-nights, illicit auctions, and- oh, I couldn't possibly list all our adventures. Sometimes we found ourselves in serious danger. Sometimes, the souls we munched on were tainted or poisonous. But, no matter what, we always stuck together."

"Oh, father," Downy swore, "Just get on with it, already."

Thunderpuss continued, oblivious. "But when we landed here, Lucien changed. He was always hungry and so obsessed. He spent every waking moment trying to figure out how to leave the Island. I tried to convince him that we should just enjoy our time here, that everything would work itself out in the long term. The Island was by far the nicest place we'd docked. I tried to tell him that it wouldn't be so bad, even if we were stuck here forever. But he wouldn't listen. Then, one day he went out hunting by himself, and came back with those wings. That's when life became unbearable.

"Almost all of the other Weres grew wings, too," Thunderpuss gestured to Cheri. "But I never did. I don't know if it was something I did or didn't do, but it stuck a wedge between Lucien and me. He started calling me fat and lazy, as if I wasn't doing enough to help him get us off this Island. He told me I was less than a person. That I was- oh I can't do this."

"Pah," Downy said. "This is useless."

189

"Hush, child!" scolded Cheri. "Come now, dear Thunderpuss, keep going. You're almost there! I can feel it. I need to hear the end of your story."

"He told me I was incomplete! That he was better off without me!" Thunderpuss sobbed. "He said that I was just trying to ride his tailfeathers. Trying to be beautiful by association! But that was the opposite of the truth! I just wanted to spend some time with him, maybe play some Hide-and-Seek or Truth-or-Dare. For old times' sake! Even Kick-the-Can would have satisfied me, but I got nothing. It was too painful to see him like that, so, I left the Mists, never to return!"

"That's terrible," Vespa murmured. "He abandoned you for no good reason! That soulless ass! If that's how he treats you, he's not good enough to be your friend."

"She's right!" I agreed. "You need friends who accept you for exactly what you are, wings or no."

"Could those friends be you guys? I promise I'll be the best friend you could ask for!"

I shrugged. Vespa nodded. Cheri patted Thunderpuss on the side of his head.

"Speak with your actions, not this sappiness. Get us to the Lucien's lair, that's all I need from you," Downy said. "Then we can go about our lives separately, just as miserable as we were before meeting."

Thunderpuss nodded, a solemn bob of the head to show he understood the pain in Downy's breast.

By dusk, all four of us had settled on Thunderpuss' broad back. He was wide enough we could sit two-by-two, and his hair was easy to grab for stabilization. The sepia Mist descended on the bog, converging on our steadfast mount. Thunderpuss walked into the closest front, and all traces the Island disappeared from view. The Mist was a perfect veil, obscuring even moonlight. I'm not sure how he was able see more than a foot in front of himself, but somehow Thunderpuss worked his way up to a steady gait. He lumbered through the Mist, his momentum carrying him through any obstacle. Most obstructions I could only detect after he trampled them, as they crumbled beneath his feet. The trees and shrubberies of the Mists (or whatever it was that grew in the land of darkness) offered no resistance to Thunderpuss' mighty mass.

Deep in the Mists, there was no way I could track our distance traveled or any way to keep the time. I tried counting time in my head, but was distracted by half-scenes evoked by the Mist. I thought I saw figures dashing about, committing atrocious acts, but everything was just obscure enough that I couldn't be sure. Lascivious nymphs chewed up suitors in a furious bacchanal. A cryptic dragon razed an imperial city to the floor. I saw a hooded stranger, more than once, forcing himself on fractured bodies, rearranging their pieces into new characters. I found the scenes unbearable to watch, but my vision was attracted to anything different from the constant brown backdrop of Mist.

It hurt to think. I couldn't determine whether the scenes I saw were the product of some process in my brain, or if the processes in my brain were the product of actual shapes in the Mist. Thunderpuss was traveling much too fast for me to move about or ask any of my friends what they thought. Instead, I let go of my thoughts and let them wander among the endless swirling tendrils. I nearly lost myself in infinite madness, my thoughts nothing more than miniscule imprints on the Mist.

Dawn broke before I lost myself completely. The warmth of sunlight embraced us, shining down from clear skies above. The Mists vanished, leaving us stranded in a pristine, grassy rectangle. Cold, grey buildings stretched into the sky, forming a tall perimeter around the verdant glen. Above the tops of the towers, a silver Winged creature screeched a warning as it soared through the atmosphere. All of this was foreign, but familiar.

Vespa grinned as wide as a canyon crack. "We did it!" she cried, "Charlie, we made it through the Mists! I'm finally home!"

OBLIVIOUS

"We made it!" Vespa leaped off Thunderpuss and embraced the ground. "Grass has never felt so good. The air has never tasted so rich. Oh, I can smell the scent of everything homey and wonderful!" Vespa jumped to her feet, poised for action. "All these sensations are bringing my memories back. I'm beginning to remember everything. Oh shit, I'm home!"

The rest of us looked around struck dumb by bludgeoning awe. The square itself was incredible. It seemed impossible that there was more to the world, hidden behind the skyscraping buildings.

"Is this where we were expecting to go?" I asked, sliding down the side of our mount. "I thought we wanted to find Lucien's fortress. I somehow imagined as looking a bit more fortress-like."

"This isn't where I meant to go at all!" Thunderpuss moaned. "Oh, bother, I can't even get myself where I need to be, the one time I really need to be there. It's no wonder I'll never have any friends."

"Oh, stop it," I said, "We'll just get back on and we'll go back into the Mists. I'm sure you'll get us there, eventually."

"Hey, Charlie, I don't know if that's going to happen for a while," Vespa said, drawing a circle in the air. "Look around. The Mist is gone!"

Sure enough, as I spun myself about, I saw that the world was sunny, not a vaporous body in sight. The Mist had dumped us out and disappeared, derailing us from our journey. I fell onto my back and stared up at this new sky. It was such a welcoming blue, spotted with inviting clouds. The cold, wet grass felt good through my shirt. The scent of palm lilies trickled into my nose. A good part of me hoped this was my home, too, and that we could just forget about our quests for a minute. Just for a few minutes.

"Well, can't we just wait here for nightfall?" I asked. "The Mist will come back. It always does."

Thunderpuss shrugged, causing Downy to tumble off his back onto soft earth. "Sorry, bird," the Were-beast said. "It's possible. Probable, even. Oh, I hope it comes back."

"Well, in the meantime, we should go to my house!" Vespa said. "I know it's unlikely, but maybe my mom found her way back here, too. I mean, if we could do it, why couldn't she? Come on, my place is just a short walk from here, and I'll make us some tea!"

I rolled onto my side, to inspect the grass beside me. The soil beneath was still damp from morning dew. A little, fuzzy worm was perched on the top of a large blade next to me. It was arching its whole body as hard as it could, trying to keep its body as far away from the damp earth as possible. Two bright orange antennae waved hello, as if he and I were old friends. I couldn't place a name to the face.

"Charlie, are you coming?" Vespa called. Our party had begun to move.

We followed Vespa's lead through the maddening urban labyrinth. As we navigated the sidewalks, we passed several other Wingless humans, who seemed to pay us no mind. They couldn't be bothered to notice a giant monster or a half-naked bird-woman traipsing down the street.

"Vespa, why are these people so oblivious to us?" I asked.

"Hey, this is the city we're talking about, after all," she replied, "Things can get pretty crazy downtown. Everyone's so wrapped up in his or her own business. They don't really give anything outside their little sphere a second thought. Nothing fazes them, as long as they get where they're going."

"And, tell me, what city is this exactly?"

"It's, you know, the City! The City is where I'm from, Charlie! Don't you pay any attention to me?"

"I'm just a little worried. Things seem a little bit more odd than usual. What if this isn't your home? What if Lucien's just playing us for saps, and this is all an illusion? He's the Warlock for crying out loud. Tricking us into thinking this is your home is within the limits of his power."

"Well, if we're here, maybe this is where we're supposed to be. Even if it's under an enchantment, maybe this is where we need to go!"

"But, ask yourself how we got here! Did you once stop to think about that?" I yelled, stopping in the middle of the sidewalk. "This place is definitely not part of the Island!"

"Obviously not. I don't remember there being any skyscrapers on the Island, unless you count the Azure Peak, which I most definitely do not!"

"And, you got trapped on the Island by falling out of an airplane! That was in the middle of an ocean! We just walked here! It's got to be connected somehow."

"Maybe so. But, contrary to your belief, I have been wondering about this. Lots," Vespa corrected, "In fact, I've got myself some solid theories. I've been thinking that maybe I came upon the Island through the Mists. Maybe you did, too. Maybe our memories were the only things that couldn't make it past the vapors. Now that I'm back here, most of mine have rushed back to me. I'm just missing a few, unimportant details like the name of the City. That doesn't really matter. This place is still the City where I was born. It makes sense that if we go back through the Mists to wherever you're from, your memories will come back, yeah?"

"No, it doesn't make sense!" I snapped. "How can we be in a city off the Island if the Mists aren't allowed to leave the Island."

"Since when can't they do that?"

"It's in the Rules! They can't move over water. They can't go above a certain altitude. That's why the mountainfolk moved up into the cliffs! They're safe because the Mists can't reach them!"

Vespa shook her head. "I don't know of any Rules like that, Charlie."

"Downy!" I pleaded, "You're the one who first told me those secrets. Tell me now that I'm not crazy!"

"I don't know what to say," said Downy. "I don't know what you're talking about."

"Oh, this is preposterous!" I shouted. "How could I be forgetting so much? You're all mad! There are Rules! The Mist can't attack the same place twice! Come on, you guys!"

"Look, I'll tell you what, Charlie. Let's just take a breath and keep on walking to my house. Once we get there, I'll be able to tell you for certain whether or not this is my home. Maybe Lucien has a good guess as to what the City looks like, but he can't know all the details of my personal life. We'll take a peek inside my diary, all right?"

Too shaken to stir, I agreed through silence.

Vespa led us through a few more turns and stopped at a human-sized doorway at the base of a skyscraping edifice.

"Go ahead, I'll stay outside with Thunderpuss to make sure he doesn't get himself lost," Cheri offered.

"Well, I'll stay outside to make sure you two Were-folk don't get any ideas about up and leaving us," Downy muttered. "Be quick, you two."

Vespa and I entered the tower and raced up a spiral staircase, located at the center of the lobby. We scaled four floors, each composed of a small landing with two apartments facing each other. On the fifth level, Vespa exited the stairwell and turned to the door on our left. A quick rap earned no response, so Vespa turned the handle and the door swung in on its hinges.

The sweeping entry revealed a quaint living room, furnished by two sofas draped with doilies. Paintings of farms lined the walls, and a short easel was erected in one corner. Behind it, I saw a stack of untouched canvasses. A small corridor led to more rooms and a kitchen was annexed to the living area.

Vespa placed her hands on her hips in victory. "Yes, this is exactly how I remember it! Need more proof? Dad's safe should be behind the third painting, there. The one with the sheep grazing out front." I walked over to remove the scenic portrait, per my mistress' orders. Up close, I could tell the piece had been painted with great care by thousands of tiny, delicate brushstrokes. Each lamb, however tiny, was the product of an intense passion for aesthetic.

"Vespa, did you paint this? The brushwork is amazing."

"No, painting was always my father's deal. He tried to get me into it, but I was never any good at it."

"What about your mother? Was she an artist?"

"Sure, you could say so. She made both of these." Vespa gestured to the doilies. "Every night, she crocheted her time away. Huh. That's funny."

"What's so funny?"

"Well, I just remembered. She and my father split up years ago. She left us to fend for ourselves while she moved to another city to try and succeed in the doily industry. I guess if you spend enough time with yarn, it's bound to make you a bit wound up, huh?"

"What? That's not even a little bit funny. Why would you joke about something as depressing like that?"

"Well, I mean, it's not funny that she left us. It's just funny that I would remember that now, while we're alone in my family's apartment. But, hey, I guess that explains why Lucien captured my father, not my mother. It was only my father and I out skydiving. My mom wasn't anywhere around to get caught."

"What are you talking about? Are you getting mixed up again?"

"Ah, father, mother. Airplane, skydive. Whatever."

"Aren't you going to be at least a little bit upset? This is sad news we just rediscovered!"

"No, it's not news. She was out of my life before I found my way to the Island, I just forgot about it. I'm telling you, those Mists are memory nets. It seems like everything important gets filtered out. Who knows what else I'll remember? Hey, maybe my memories of those Rules or whatever got trapped back on the Island side of the Mists? I don't know, Charlie. Standing around this old apartment makes me feel exhausted. Come on, there's nothing to help us here."

"What about your diary? Don't you want to make sure this is the real City? What if this is a trap?"

"No, I'm sure it's the real deal, now. I've seen enough. Go ahead and check that safe, though. Combination 36-24-36. My dad was a real ladies man. It's no wonder that my mom left. He was just a stupid artist, using his skills to get into the pants of his fans."

"Geez, I believe you. I've heard enough. I trust your instincts. I'm okay with leaving now."

We walked back out of her apartment when an intoxicating scent filled my nose. My stomach began to roar like Thunderpuss, begging me for attention. I hallucinated an odor trail, light blue and glittering, leading to the door at the opposite side of the landing.

"Vespa, hold on a second," I said, "I feel like we should check this out. It could be important. Or delicious. Deliciously important."

I saw Vespa licking her lips, smacking them in accordance. She walked over to the door and rapped one time. The door swung in on its hinges.

"Hello? Is there anybody in here?" she inquired. "We're from next door and we wanted to know if we could, um, invite you to have dinner tonight? We're trying to get to know our neighbors a little better."

"Oh, come in! Please, make yourselves comfortable! I'll be with you in a moment," said the unseen chef, from the apartment's kitchen. "However, I'm afraid I must decline your offer. I've already prepared a meal, you see."

"Is that so? This delectable odor is coming from your apartment? I had no idea!" Vespa lied. "It smells so marvelous. What is it that you're making?"

We crept inside to find a living room decorated in stark contrast to the one in Vespa's abode. Here, the space was crammed with all sorts of furniture. Six couches of varying sizes combined into a mosaic of comfort. A variety of dressers and shelf units lined the walls, stacked with an onomatopoeia of kitsch.

"Oh, nothing too fancy, just some garlic mashed potatoes, some marinated, braised turkey, some blanched asparagus, and I'm about to put in the pear cobbler." A pie dish screeched as it slid into

201

the center of an oven rack. The unseen speaker revealed himself, still adorned with oven mitts. "Well, if it isn't little Miss Dvorak. I didn't recognize your voice. My, how you've grown!"

Our gracious host was a muscular human about three inches taller than me. His skin tone was dark, darker than me by at least three shades. His hair fell in tight spirals down to his broad shoulders, framing a grin at least three times as bright as my own. It amplified his mystery at least twenty-seven times. The man was also Wingless.

"I'm sorry, you must have me confused for someone else," Vespa said. "I don't believe we've met."

"No, I'm sure it's you. Velma, right? Nespa? No, Vespa!"

"That's right! Sorry, but how do you know me again?"

"Well, no other family produces such fabulously fuchsia hair. Oh, and I used to spend a fair bit of time with your mom. Cooking! Yes, we would cook together. Several meals a day, sometimes. She told me about you and showed me pictures of you in your baby booties, but she never let me meet you. So, don't feel bad about not recognizing me. We've never met! My name's Marlon, by the way."

"Ha! All right, then, how do you do, Marlon?" Vespa asked.

"Frankly, my dear, I'm famished," Marlon said with a wink, "Please, join me. Let's eat before this dinner gets cold."

We ate like monsters, swallowing chunks of meat whole and slurping down their juices. I carved the turkey, Vespa speared the asparagus, and Marlon reamed the potatoes. The food was so far beyond delicious my taste buds couldn't register individual flavors. Birdseed and creamed ice had been my staple foods for so long that anything else I ate was a message from the unknown spirit, a reminder that I might try to pray to him on occasion. Yes, the meal was so good it made me a believer!

OPHIDIAN

Once the heat of the feast dissipated, the room chilled faster than I anticipated.

"Gosh, Vespa, I'm sorry to bring up that old stew of emotions, about me and your mom," Marlon started, "I'm sure it's a tender subject."

"It's all right. I figured you weren't just cooking together. I mean, my dad wasn't the most faithful husband. I'm happy that my mother was finding happiness in her own way."

"Hey! It's not that your parents didn't savor each other! No, they loved one another, hot as a crock-pot. No bones about it."

"No, I understand. If they didn't love each other, they wouldn't have been able to love me like they did. I just mean, I'm glad they were able to find complete satisfaction during their time together. You take it where you find it, wherever it lies, no?"

"Right, but-"

"And then, when you're no longer getting everything you need, you move along until you find it somewhere else."

"Wait a minute, what's that supposed to mean?"

"Well, my mother wasn't getting what she wanted from my father, so she came to you. But when you let her down, well, she couldn't handle sticking around any longer."

"You're blaming me for your mother's disappearance? Now, that's just plain ridiculous! If you've got some beef with me, then let it out to graze. Don't marinate the hate!"

"Hey, I'm going to go check on Cheri and Downy and Thunderpuss," I interjected, maneuvering towards the door. "We've been up here a lot longer than we said we would be. I don't want them to worry about us."

"Sure, sure," Vespa said, waving me away like an annoying gnat. "Do whatever you feel is necessary. I'm busy at the moment."

"Are you going to come down soon?"

Vespa patted her gut. "I'm so stuffed, I'm not moving for a little while. Bye for now."

"Fine, I'll come get you if the sky starts showering us with molten rocks or the zombie apocalypse gets its legs on the ground. How about that?"

"Yeah, okay. Sure! Whatever! Go do your thing!"

I turned with a huff and puffed out the door, slamming it behind me. I was about to storm down the stairwell when something caught my eye. The door to Vespa's apartment was ajar, ever so slightly cracked, though I was sure we had shut it on leaving. I walked over to investigate.

"Hello?" I asked. "Is there anybody here?"

I knocked once before entering, as seemed to be the custom in these parts. There was nobody in the living room, nobody in the kitchen. I saw, resting on one of the couches, the painting of the sheep farm. Naked on the wall, Vespa's family vault remained shut, its innards still protected from the world. I unlocked the safe and pried it open. The cube itself contained nothing, but the chamber's back wall was missing. In its place was an opening leading into another room.

I crammed myself through the safe and fell into the secret chamber on the other side. No windows or doors offered me escape; safe passage was the only way in or out. Aside from its lack of portals, the room appeared to be an ordinary children's room. The bed was shaped like a sports car and had dragster print on its sheets. Model parts covered a desk. A half-complete convertible weighed down a small book. As I moved to grab the book, I heard the safe door thud shut behind me. I spun on my heels, rushed to the wall, and rapped on the inner wall of the safe.

"Hey, you trapped me in here! Didn't you see that there's someone in here! Hey! Don't just walk away"

I gave up trying to make noise. The safe was made of thick material. My voice couldn't carry through it. All the banging quickly bruised my hands.

"If I wait just a bit, surely whoever shut me in will come back. It was probably just Vespa checking up on things. Maybe she felt bad about sending me away with such terse words. She probably didn't notice me in here, but she'll figure out that I'm missing. Surely, she'll realize that I'm stuck behind those old sheep," I tried to tell myself. I wasn't convincing.

As the air grew stagnant, claustrophobia gnawed at the edges of my vision. An obsessive compulsion to escape swelled in all of my muscles. I determined I would pass time as quickly as possible by staying as busy as possible. First and foremost, I knew I had to finish the model on the desk. Hundreds of pieces later, I found myself in the same situation, but with a beautiful hot rod to keep me company.

Bored, I picked up the book from the table and flipped through it, absorbing its contents like they were my own memories:

August

I finally understand what they mean by "the summer of love." Three months in and I'm still aflutter. If I didn't know better I'd say I had arrhythmia, the way my heart skips beats. Just the thought of him sends me into a fatal love-spiral. He makes me want to do the stupidest things. I want to build us a castle out of pancakes. I want to prank call his mother. I want to draw his naked body in crayons. I want to draw on his naked body in crayons. I want to leap off a cliff holding hands. I want to do it all and then some! With him, I know I can imagine anything into reality! Life is such a grand adventure!

September

Do you remember? The way he held you down, the way he ruled your every waking moment? The way he became your everything? Well, now he is less than nothing. Nega-nothing! He crossed a line that was not meant to be crossed. There isn't any way to step back over, once you've gone that far. He made it more real than anything I've ever known! Too real. Unbelievable fantasy turned to a nightmare. I can't do it again. I can't handle the strain on my heart. The juxtaposition of my needs and desires is much too intense. He must be cut from my life.

October

As autumn settles in, how hard I must fall! Not once, but twice, in a year do I change my foliage? I'm a lucky one to have such tenacious branches. I'm wrapped in his snuggling embrace once more. He proved me wrong. I was sure it couldn't be done, but he reminded me why I first fell for him. Fantasy and reality may not only coexist, they are meant to intermingle beautifully. The line has faded away, almost completely. Our fantastic and mundane have bled together to the point where they are indistinguishable. If you asked me a few months ago, I would have said this situation could never be. It would bother me too much. But really, it's pretty great. I am satisfied.

November

It could be that I've finally found my meaning. My place is by his side, not behind or beneath him. Our perfect kingdom is nearly complete. Rather, it was complete from the moment we met, considering that we are its monarchs. Well, no, it is even better now. A different kind of complete. It has been refined and purified. We have achieved perfect balance with each other and everything. I can't imagine a weapon powerful enough to topple our fortress. Together, we are invulnerable, impervious.

December

And, apparently, oblivious. How did I miss that coming? This time I mean it! This time my word is strong as tempered steel. Never again will I turn a tender heart to that tainted love. I can't stand to feel it rent asunder, gnawed by the teeth of a nasty gentleman. I'll secede from the world, sleep in my womb and heal these wounds. I refuse to face another year of the same, lukewarm cycle. I feel myself whirling into dementia. There's no rhyme for me to follow, no reason to check my flag. I'm done.

The remaining pages were wordless but full, covered in primitive, charcoal doodles. The first few scenes were nothing more than scribbles, nightmare serpents knotting their bodies into monstrous, writhing planets. Over the next few pages, the view panned back, revealing the circles to be negative eyes at the peak of a pallid face. The artist's blunt rubbing technique accented the character's angular features, igniting a cold fire in his stare. The final page revealed Lucien in his complete, necrotic glory, arms spread wide to embrace the reader and welcome him to the billowing folds of the Mist.

OBVIOUS

I ran over to the safe and pounded on the inside of the door again. To my surprise, the door opened after my first solid rap. I scrambled through the passage and ran across the hall to Marlon's apartment. I entered the apartment to find Vespa and her mother's lover hugging and weeping over the empty pear cobbler dish.

"What's happening?"

"Oh, Charlie! I have the best news," Vespa said, smiling through her tears. "I think I know where my father is."

"Really? That's great! Can Marlon help us find him?"

"No, Charlie! He is my father."

I shook my head. "No, don't be ridiculous. You can't be serious. You're not serious, are you?"

"It turns out that he and my mother started seeing each other right when I was conceived! Nine months later I came stumbling out and they started seeing a bit less of each other."

"It's true," Marlon laughed. "I guess that might explain why your mother never let me see you, Vespa. She was afraid I might recognize you as the fruit of my own loins. That might have spoiled things for her and your dad."

Vespa nodded. "Not that things didn't go sour anyway."

"I'm just a little bit skeptical," I started.

"Don't be. Check it out, Charlie. We've both got the same color eyes, the same number of teeth, and the same birthmark on our thighs. Look, it's a pear. If that doesn't make it the truth, then I'm not sure what will."

"I'm not so sure that's how these things work," I said. "Look, Vespa. I was just over in your apartment and I read a book I found. A diary of some kind."

"You read my diary without asking me? How dare you!"

"I'm sorry! I was trapped in a strange room with no doors. You never told me that your place was so strange. What I mean to say is that it seemed like the right thing to do at the time."

"What did you see?"

"Lucien! Lucien took over the second half of the book. He was drawn over and over, smaller and smaller."

"Oh, you're preposterous. You expect me to believe that I drew pictures of Lucien in my childhood diary?"

"No, Vespa! You're not getting me. This place isn't real! It's a trap set by Lucien to make us forget our mission. We're too close to achieving whatever goal he's so afraid we'll reach."

"Oh, stop it!" Vespa snapped. "You're just jealous that I'm spending time with my father instead of with you. Now that we're safe, we don't have to stick together every moment. Deal with it. Make yourself comfortable, we'll be here a while."

I was too irate for her words to damage me the way she intended. " You can just forget about our adventures just like that? Look, when we first arrived, I felt that this place was very nice. Too nice. In fact, for a moment, I even hoped it was my real home. But, after what I just saw, I'm sure this is a deception! Lucien is a cruel, cruel man! Are you so excited by this fake nostalgia that you can abandon our mission off-hand? You're so selfish."

The color drained from Vespa's pale face, taking her skin a shade beyond bleached death. "Whether or not you're right, Charlie, my feelings are real. I've finally found my real father and now you want to separate us from each other? Perhaps Lucien is not the cruelest man I know."

"Vespa, are you hearing me at all? Look, if this is what you need, if this is what you want, then stay. I'm going to continue on with our original goal of defeating Lucien. I don't think you should stay here. It's not safe! And, more importantly, I want you to come with me."

"Oh, yes, and I'm the selfish one? I don't think so, Charlie. You're just projecting the worst parts of yourself onto me and onto Lucien. I know he's our enemy, but still."

"What did Marlon put in that food to make you so ridiculous? You won't listen to me and you're ignoring our friends outside. It's like we

213

don't matter at all, anymore. That's criminal narcissism."

"You're out of line!" Vespa snapped. "I've got back what Lucien took from me. I'm allowed to savor this little bit of happiness."

Her blunt words cut me in a way I'd never felt. It was worse pain than any jungle plant could inflict. This spell would make me bleed to death without a tourniquet. "Fine. Stay here. Downy, Cheri, Thunderpuss, and I will continue on to fight the Warlock. We'll go retrieve my reflection and avenge Downy's murdered family, all on our own. Your sass will just- oh, never mind. Goodbye, Vespa."

I struck a sympathetic nerve. "I didn't mean, I didn't want," Vespa blushed, flustered by her verbal frustration.

"Sweetie, you didn't mention your quest for revenge," Marlon said, "You've got to go and finish your battle, before that fire inside you dies. You're nubile and passionate! Serve your vengeance while it's still hot. Be a chef that your father can be proud of."

"You're right," Vespa said. "I should finish what I started. Nobody likes to be cut off mid-course."

"No," I said, "I don't want you to come because you feel like you ought to do this. I want you to come because you want to be there beside us."

"You're right, Charlie. This was important to me, and to my friends. It still is. We've got to do this. We're so close. I'm," Vespa stuttered and blushed. "I'm embarrassed."

"It's okay. I just want to know, what were you thinking?"

"I don't know," Vespa said. "I was just doing what felt right."

"Hmm, that sounds familiar."

"I'm sorry! Whatever! I just lost track of the time, and, with it, my mind."

"Well, it's nearly dusk," said Marlon, scratching his ear. "I don't want to keep you in any later than I already have. I don't want to make things any harder."

"No, it's all right!" Vespa insisted. "I've just got to go take care of something. I promise, once this is all over, I'll come back and we'll make up for lost time. Okay, Dad?"

She ran over and embraced the man she hadn't known existed before a few hours ago.

I coughed to break the awkward silence. "Come on, we'd best get down to our friends. They're probably worried about us, if they haven't decided to just murder each other out of boredom."

Vespa nodded, grabbed my hand, and dragged me out the door before Marlon started up crying again. She stopped at the top of the staircase. "Charlie, I'm sorry I snapped at you. This place is where I was born and raised, but it isn't my home. It hasn't been my home for a long while now. And this vision of it, well, it's extra weird. What happened in Marlon's apartment, well, I was scared. I was just clinging to something that felt like home."

"Do you think Lucien sent us here? Was this detour a red herring, or do you believe that guy is your father?"

"It's possible. I mean, I'd like to believe he's my father. He cooks the most delicious food I've ever imagined."

"I'll give him that."

"I can't say for certain, but I think things are in motion that Lucien has no control over. I'm pretty certain that whatever he's afraid of is already underway and he has no idea how it's going to pan out. I would bet a lot of money we're smack dab in the middle of something epic."

"A tempest of some sort, right?"

"Yeah, sure. Whatever you want to call it, Charlie."

"Either way, he's pulling out the big guns. These spells that he's using on us are powerful, but subtle. I didn't even know he was enchanting us until it was too late. He just wanted up to stop here and forget everything."

"It's true, I think. He's a damn powerful Warlock."

"It's a good thing that we've got a powerful enchantress on our side, huh?"

"Who's that?" Vespa asked.

"Well, you are, aren't you? All those spells you cast on me when we first met. Freezing my tongue, mashing up my brain, making my heart speed up way too fast. Those are some real potent spells you've got in your arsenal."

Vespa laughed her tinkling chuckle and kissed me on the cheek.

"Come on, Charlie, those silly friends of us are probably really worried."

We descended the spiral stairs, holding hands. Each turn of the coil wound our grasp a little bit tighter.

STACCATO

"I swore that if you two didn't come back in the next five minutes, I was going to shave him bare," said Downy, jumping about on Thunderpuss' back. "He kept moaning and pissing about how you two were going to abandon us here forever. I mean, I wouldn't blame you for leaving this big doofbag behind."

"Except that we need him to get through the Mists," I corrected.

"Don't worry Thunderpuss," Vespa said in her most adorable baby talk, "Don't let the big scary birdie worry you! If he bothers you, you can just roll over on him in your sleep."

Downy quieted his taunting and we slipped back into the settling Mist. There was a bizarre quality to the Mist that night. It was moister than the last time we'd traveled, sticking hungrily to my skin. With every breath, an acrid specter slipped into my lungs, inflating them with burning urgency. I saw no hidden shapes dashing about, no scenes just out of my conscious sight. Everything lay still.

But, in the middle of our trek, a Mist typhoon was born.

It ripped me off the back of Thunderpuss, despite fervent attempts to grasp his flaxen hair. My probing hand encountered another just like it, and they clasped together tight before the powerful winds knocked me unconscious.

Vespa and I woke to impenetrable silence. All of our companions had gone missing. We were lost in the Mists with no clues to our location. There was no such thing as a landmark in this realm. However, one thing could I see with alarming clarity. Approximately thirty yards away stood a tall figure in a white, hooded robe.

I gestured to my companion to stay silent.

"Vespa, be very, very quiet. I know this stranger and he's a dangerous, volatile being. He comes to me in my dreams. He's done terrible, terrible things to me."

"Are you serious? He's popped up in my dreams, too," Vespa whispered. "I thought I was the only one who'd been dreaming about him. I'm glad to know I'm not alone."

"What does he do in your dreams?"

"Well, most recently, he's taken me out to the opera for my birthday celebration. Sometimes he buys me drinks at a swanky bar. Or, he'll take me on long drives through the middle of nowhere. It's always a nice, refreshing dream."

"That's lucky. He's always got me ensnared in some sort of horrible torture device. I usually wake up just as I'm about to die. Usually."

"Oh, Charlie! That's horrible! I mean, he occasionally disappears and leaves me with the bill, but that's nothing compared to dying. Why didn't you say anything to me?"

"The only nights he bothered me were the nights you weren't around. I couldn't exactly talk to you about them."

"Oh, you don't think I have anything to do with this, do you?"

"No, no! Not at all! I was just noting the coincidence. It's almost like he's afraid of you. Or he likes you."

Vespa nodded. "Well, that should make this a whole lot easier, yeah?" She shouted at the hooded man. "Hey buddy! Let's talk."

The stranger turned without moving. His body flickered and reappeared facing us, a dozen yards closer. His well-hidden mouth exhaled, blowing Mist into concentric spirals away from his hood.

"I've been expecting you," said an inorganic voice. The timbre of the stranger's voice was neither human nor bird, male nor female. There was no doubt in my ears that this person was not alive.

"Excuse me," Vespa said, "But we've managed to get ourselves separated from our friends. You wouldn't have happened to see a gigantic Thunderpuss, a falcon, or a sexy Were-lady, would you?"

"They are of no concern to me."

"And we are of no concern to you!" I said. "Come on, Vespa, let's be moving along."

"Who are you?" Vespa asked.

"I am Stranger."

"Stranger than what?"

"Everything."

"Well, Stranger, it sure is nice to meet you, at long," I said. "I've been having dreams about someone who looks just like you. Terrible nightmares, actually. Lots of torture and near-death experiences. You wouldn't happen to know anything about that, would you?"

"Yes. Those were warnings from me. You did not heed my words."

"Well, they weren't so much words as they were horrible torture contraptions, but I think I get your point. And, you know, one time you led me to safety. You showed me the way to the Azure Egress."

"I was trying to lead you away from the girl. You left her side, but you were still together. That was an unacceptable situation."

"What does that mean? Why do you care? You know, it seems like lots of people have been trying to split us up. Why is that? Tell me, what were you trying to warn me about?"

"You have many questions. I cannot answer them to your satisfaction. I tried to warn you away from this place. I cannot allow you to travel any further in this direction or the world, as you know it, will end. Vespa's world will be destroyed as well.

I am trying to protect her and her world by sending you away. I tried to warn you, I did. You did not listen. Now, I must stop you by dire means."

"Oh really? Well, how exactly did you plan on doing that?" Vespa asked. "There are two of us here. We can totally take down your lonesome Were-ass. Right, Charlie?"

"Um," I said, "I'm not exactly sure what you expect me to do. This guy, he has so many weapons. I don't even have my bowl anymore."

"He's only a threat in your dreams!" Vespa said. "Those are just illusions, right?"

"Yes, but I thought he was just a dream, and he's real now. So, that's not any consolation," I muttered. "Stranger, how am I going to end the world by going deeper into the Mists? I'm not going to hurt anything, I promise! Just Lucien, maybe a couple more Weres, if I have to. Look, who are you really? Can't we compromise?"

"I need only stop you, Wingless boy. The girl may do as she sees fit. This is her world, and you must not be allowed to destroy it!"

"That's retarded. You're not making sense, dude," Vespa said, "And, there's no way we're splitting up. We promised to stick together. Besides, if I can do as I see fit, I want to go with this boy to find my friends. We're on our way to fight the Warlock. Who are you to try and stop us?"

After a moment of heavy breathing, Stranger raised his sleeve to his face and threw back his hood. There was nothing inside the robe but Mist.

"I am the Mists at the edge of your mind, my lady. I am the border that guards your heartland. And I shall not let that boy slip past me."

Stranger raised an arm above his vacant headspace. A whorl of Mist accumulated near his sleeve opening. He threw his arm forward, as though he were tossing a ball. Tendrils of Mist shot from his sleeves, snaking towards me. As they hissed closer, static charge built up, drawing them tight and hypnotizing me into paralysis. I watched the weapon race towards me as my legs turned to concrete. Just before impact, Vespa shoved me out of its path.

The whips of Mist stuck her in the chest and then wrapped themselves around her arms and thighs. The static charge coursed through her body, spiking all of her synapses. She wailed a blend of pain and pleasure as all of her neurotransmitters released at once. With a solid tug on the Mist whip, Stranger forced Vespa to her knees.

I scrambled to my feet and ran to her side. "Vespa, give me your hand. Get up!"

"Stop! Charlie, just run! There's nothing you can do against him!" Vespa yelled. "He'll make us both suffer. I can't bear to see you hurt. Please! Escape while you have the chance."

The terror in her eyes belied her fear. I placed my hand on her shoulder. "No, there's no way I could live with myself if I were to leave you here right now. Remember, we promised each other we'd never be part again. Don't worry, I'll save you."

As I uttered my pledge of bravery, a second serving of electricity coursed its way through the Mist-whips, through Vespa's slender frame, up my arm, and through all the connections in my brain. I swallowed one last gasp of burning vapor before collapsing under the weight of an astral rainbow.

LEGATO

"Everything is so slow!" I said, to no one in particular. "The creatures, the grass, the dancing birds. Why, it even feels like the air itself has decided to quit playing in standard time. I feel like I'm stuck in a film. I've got no control over anything!"

You've got no control over anything, a voice echoed, directly in my brain. Colors still swirled before my eyes, obscuring the speaker's identity along with whatever reality I was facing.

"Vespa, are you there? Where are you? What happened to her? Is she all right?"

Is she right? the voice paraphrased. *Can you trust her? Can she trust you?*

"Of course she's right. What an absurd question! Ha! I trust her. She's always right."

She's right there. Right before you, behind you, beside you. Always. Can't you feel her?

"Right where? I can't see anything. Is there anything you can do to help me get my vision back to normal? Look, I'm desperate, whoever you are! Is there any way?"

Who are you, anyway? Do you really know?

"That's what I'm asking you! What do you gain by keeping me here? I don't know who you are, but I don't think you know what you're doing here."

What are you doing here? You don't understand your purpose.

"Let me be free! I don't belong to you!"

You don't belong. Not here. Not anywhere.

"That's not what I meant at all! Now, tell me what happened to that white-robed Stranger and the pink-haired girl. Where is my friend?"

Is she your friend? Just your friend? Why is she your friend and just your friend?

"Give me an answer already! I'm tired of all your questions! I want to see again! Help me! Make the real world appear!"

Taste a pear. It's in your pocket.

I reached into my pants for the lumpy fruit and gnawed a big bite out of it. It tasted so familiar, like a palm lily soaked in homemade wine. The random colors dispersed and left me stranded on the floor of a large stone room filled with ramshackle, ancient pews. The ceiling was raised high by grand arches, set around stained glass portraits. Hundreds of thousands of fragments of glass combined to form a mosaic of forgotten gods, angels of feathered wings. Rainbow lights filtered down to icons carved in the floor, tinting everything with a bizarre palette.

At the far end of the hall, a sweeping staircase crept up to the second story of the cathedral. A dark red carpet spilled down its center like blood from a fresh kill. At the peak of the stairs stood Lucien in a familiar pose, arms stretched wide to embrace me. Just as my vision settled enough to focus, he swept down the stairs to dance with my aching body.

FORTISSIMO

"You made it to the end of your journey, my boy. Congratulations and accolades are deserved, to be sure. Whatever shall you do next?" Lucien boomed, his voice echoing through the empty hall.

"Kill you, most likely," I said.

"Oh, my. Do you think you're ready? Are you prepared for what that entails? I doubt you've got the verve."

"Maybe not, but I'll do whatever it takes to knock you off your righteous pedestal. I'm so lost I've got nothing left to lose. In fact, I think I can't lose at all. So, I hope you're ready for what you've got coming, you worm."

"That's the best insult you could deliver? I want my money back. I mean, sure, thinking on your feet doesn't seem like your strong suit, but I'd hoped for something with a little more zest."

"All my friends are gone, thanks to your stupid game. I'll call you whatever I like, and then I'm going to pummel you into obscurity."

"Ooh! There's my spice."

"Before I crush you into dust, I have one question."

"Shoot, kid."

"What did you want with my reflection? Why did you steal away my facade?"

"Well, that's simple, my boy," Lucien laughed. "Even though it's two questions. The answers are: I wanted it for myself."

"But it doesn't make any sense! It's my reflection! It doesn't do you any good!"

"Charlie, Charlie, calm your little heart. You've tracked me down. That's impressive. The least I could do is to offer you a glimpse of your old self, so you can be sure you're still okay." Lucien pulled a palm-sized vanity mirror out of his pocket. "Here, here, have a look," he said, tossing me the glass, "But I've got to ask a question. Did I steal your reflection, or did you steal mine?"

I caught the small vanity and screed its dark surface. Looking out from the other side of the glass, I saw a visage at once familiar and foreign. From the same pale, chiseled face, the eyes of my enemy looked at me from within my palms. Our big ears spiraled up into the same dark horns. The only difference between my reflection and Lucien was my lack of wings.

"What is this?" I roared. "Do you think I'm joking? I'm going to destroy you, Warlock."

I tried to rush at my foe, but my feet stuck to the ground. Lucien held me captive with his gaping eyes. I was lost spelunking their endless depths. "Oh, Charlie. You're missing the point, the grand revelation this discovery should bring. You see, I am as much a part of you as you are of me. I didn't steal your reflection. I am your reflection. Or, perhaps, you are mine. I'm still undecided on the matter. What matters more is that from the moment we first met, the enemy you imagined was none other than yourself. We are partners. We are brothers. We are one and the same."

"You are lying! That's impossible. You want to get my guard down so I'll stop attempting to destroy you. I'm so many steps ahead of you, Warlock. You won't sabotage my mission!"

"No, no, no. You're so dense that I don't want to believe we're related, either. Alas, the truth is irrefutable. Charlie, I'm not going to sabotage your mission because our missions are identical."

"Don't be an ass. You're just trying to confuse me. My objective is your destruction. I want to avenge my friends, for all the atrocities you have committed against them. Your goals are to consume souls and destroy the Island. We have opposite agendas."

"Why, may I ask, are you so sure about that?"

I sputtered, out of verbal ammunition. "Well, I just am. Are you paying any attention? Didn't I just say that we're at odds? I'm trying to kill you. Surely, you don't want to let me get away with that."

Lucien shrugged. "Well, sometimes things aren't as simple as they seem. What if, by destroying me, you unwittingly destroy everything you care about? What if killing me euthanizes your own plans, hmm?"

"But you're a parasite! A pox! A plague on the world! I'm going to save the Island from you putrid hands! I'll inoculate it by vaccinating against your incurable pretentiousness."

I broke free from Lucien's binding aura and threw the mirror in a direct arc at his head. He calmly snatched it out of the air but was distracted for just long enough. I dashed alongside the vanity and used the opening to strike Lucien on the chin with a leaping punch. My knuckles connected to his jawbone, smacking against his skin with a dry crunch, hidden in echoes. I watched him step back, startled, as a ringing whorl filled my senses.

"Now do you believe me, boy?" Lucien asked, spitting pink foam over his shoulder. "We're one and the same. Reflections."

I tried to speak, but spiraling lights were making me nauseous. "I- I-"

"It's not just you, Charlie. It's everyone on the Island. They all wanted power, for one reason or another. The fat Mola wanted power and respect. The gnarly Seer wanted wisdom and safety. I'm a generous man, so I offered them all these things and more at cheaper than retail value. In exchange, I took their reflections."

"You took everybody's reflection?"

"Or their shadows. Their auras. Whatever made them an individual entity. I made a deal with just about every last creature on the Island. Those who were too proud to give me their reflections I fed to my Were-beasts. Everybody else became part of me as I became part of them. Every chin on the

Island is feeling that punch you landed. Now, just imagine what will happen if you kill me."

The thought was too tragic for me to hold in my head. Visions of dead egresses and sprawling albatrosses flickered in and out of my head. I regretted my next words before I could even process what I meant to say; yet, somehow they spilled out. "And if I were to kill one of them?"

"Oh, boy. See, we are not so different. You're just as clever and devious as I'd hoped. That, dear Charlie, is a very curious question." Lucien clapped his hands twice and Cheri entered the room, carrying before her a motionless brown mass of feathers. "Why don't we do an experiment to find out the answer?"

A lump in my throat almost stopped me from calling out his name. "Downy! Cheri, let him go! What have you done?"

"Tsk, don't worry so much," Lucien said, "He's fine, for the next few minutes at least. I'm couldn't find any other Island residents on such short notice. And Cheri can't hear you, so don't bother trying to talk her out of anything. Once a Were-beast returns to the Mists, she returns her will to her master. Oh! Those Rules can be so inconvenient at times like these. Or convenient, if you're me."

"Don't you dare touch Downy! I won't let you! I'll kill myself first! If your theory is right, you'll be dead as well. What do you think, shall we let that be our cxperiment?"

"Oh, how noble! Such selflessness makes me weak in the knees! You're a powerful soul, Charlie. I'm proud that we're reflections."

"All right Lucien, that's enough. Let my friend go," I said, picking up the hand mirror from where it had fallen in our scuffle. "My companions and I did what you asked. We tracked down all three things you took from us. You promised us a weapon to defeat you, not new age nonsense. You promised to give us the secret to your weakness and a tool to defeat you."

"Ah, but there is a catch that you're ignoring."

"Of course. Tell us about your secret loophole."

"Well, my fine reflection, the problem is that we both still exist. In truth, only one of us can be the reflection of the other. In other words, because you have not yet murdered me, you haven't reclaimed me as your own. Your reflection still belongs to me, Charlie, and I won't be giving it up easily. The only way to defeat me is to defeat me. It is quite an elegant trap, isn't it? Now, aren't you glad we played this game?"

"I'm never quite sure if you're jesting."

"Everything I do is a joke of some kind. You'll see what I mean, sooner or later. But, back to business! Whatever are you going to do about this poor falcon friend of yours? He looks absolutely wrecked! Don't worry; I cast a spell on him, so he won't feel your knife in his back. I've got to wonder, is it a reflection of the same knife that murdered his family?"

I let my body sag, exhausted by Lucien's poor humor. "Warlock, I feel sorry for you. You think everything is a joke, so you can't enjoy anything. What a sorry existence you lead."

"You're right," Lucien said, sobbing like a Siren. "Oh, god, you're right. I've never been able to forge a meaningful connection with the world. Every day, I just try and crack a smile by looking for laughs wherever I can find them, whatever the cost! Alas, my perfect grin is just a mask I wear to hide my inner demons. They're the ones who make me do such bad, bad things. They're the ones who leave me so unfulfilled with the day to day. Oh, I wish I had the strength to fight them off. But I'm so tired of fighting. So very tired. I wish you would just destroy me now and put the world out of its inane misery."

"Just kidding?" I asked.

Lucien's face snapped back to his typical evil grin. "Bingo, baby. You're on fire tonight, Charlie. I like the warmth of that flame. See, I do manage to enjoy some things. But, I know that spark is just getting started. We've got a lot to discuss, you sizzling whelp. Speaking of hot young things, where is that companion of yours? I don't want her to miss the show, the big reveal of my ultimate plan and unstoppable power."

"She's not coming. She's lost," I choked. "I think she's hurt."

"Who's not coming, Charlie?" Vespa asked, slipping into view at the top of the stairs. "I've been right beside you all this time. You didn't think that I'd really let you keep all this revenge for yourself, did you?"

Happiness welled up in my throat, clearing the clog of sorrow.

"Well, well. This is unexpected," Lucien mused, "But should make things interesting. You must have a great power inside you, dirty little witch, to avoid destruction, alone in the Mists."

"Oh, no you'd best not have just called me a dirty witch," Vespa said. "There are a lot of things I can tolerate, but calling me a witch is not allowed. If anything, I'm a sorceress, you piece of shit. And, it's about time I showed you a thing or two about real magic."

Vespa leaped from the top of the stairs and flew.

CTRL

I couldn't believe it at first. Her elegant glide was too smooth, too easy, too surreal. Then, I saw light reflect off of her nascent wings.

The wings sprouted off of Vespa's shoulders, prisms so transparent I thought they might tear if I stared too long. They grew brighter as she flew, drawing strength from the ether around her. Vespa sped toward Lucien, arms extended before her like a super-human. She clenched her hands around his neck and tackled him to the ground. Before he could catch his breath, she began pummeling him with open-fist chops. My body registered each of her blows as though she was hitting me instead of our foe. However, my joy at seeing her made each chop feel as distant as the horizon. She could beat him forever, for all I cared.

"Stop it, you pretty gnat!" Lucien shouted. With Vespa attached to his chest, pounding away, Lucien forced himself to his feet. "Get off!" He spun around, faster and faster, until Vespa was ripped off of him by raw physical force. With a quick flap of her wings, she floated over to me and landed.

"That's enough playing for now," the Warlock mumbled. "I want answers and I want them now!"

"You want answers?" Vespa piped. "Oh, I've got some answers for you, buddy."

Vespa charged at Lucien, flapping her wings to a gain a quick burst of speed. Lucien braced himself to parry, but Vespa popped into nothingness. She reappeared behind Lucien's right shoulder with her arm poised to chop. Her fist connected to his temple and he bent over double.

This was too much for my body to handle. I fell to my knees and cried out.

"Charlie!" Vespa yelped. "Are you all right? What did Lucien do to you?"

I gasped for air but couldn't form words.

"Perhaps you should have staked out the situation before rushing in so boldly," Lucien muttered, massaging his mangled limbs. "You don't know the truth about what's happening here today, do you?"

"I've got a whole load of truths safe in my hands," Vespa countered. "And I'm going to give you proof that they're right."

"Yes, but do you have the true Truth? The whole Truth? Nothing but the Truth? Can you tell me why we have gathered here today? You, me, and my reflection?"

"My reflection!" I coughed. "You're nothing but my reflection! It's not the other way around."

"Oh, bother," Lucien rolled his eyes, "My point is that Seer saw a maelstrom of chaos arriving at the Island. Do you have any idea what she was referring to, or should I just finish you off right now? I'm a mite weary of dealing with you soulful children."

"Oh, yes. I know the answer to that," Vespa said, "But I won't tell you."

"What if I were to kill your friend?" Lucien gestured to Cheri, who was now holding Downy with a knife at his gullet. "One signal and he's done. Do you think you can save him before that knife moves a half-a-hair deeper? And what do you think will happen when his blood is spilled? Will it kill me? If it kills me, well, it will surely kill old Charlie. Everything done to me is done to him. To every beast on the Island!"

"Charlie, is this true? I'm not sure I should believe him," Vespa asked, her delicate eyebrows raised.

"Vespa, it's all right! Just do it and don't worry about me! Stop Lucien now! He's mad! He claims to own the identity of every creature on the Island. He wants too much power."

Vespa's muscles twitched, her feet fidgeted against the ground. Her body couldn't decide what it was thinking, but her heart was set in boldface. "No, Charlie. There's no way I'm risking your life. Nothing could be worth that. I'm just happy to see you one more time."

"And I've never been so glad in my whole time alive. But, how did you escape? How did you survive against that sadistic demon?"

"It was easy, Charlie. I woke up."

"What are you talking about?"

"Charlie. I woke up from that terrible nightmare. Now, I'm better. This is a good dream."

"I don't understand. You can't just wake from a poor situation to find yourself a better reality. That doesn't make sense."

"It does if I'm asleep. Charlie, I'm dreaming."

"Oh, shut up. If you're dreaming, then what am I doing here?"

"I don't know, Charlie. I don't know. But, I'm glad that you're here."

Lucien smacked himself on the brow. "Of course! It all makes such sense. And yes, I'm still here, listening close. You two lovers need to remember there's a world outside your little bubble. Sometimes, it suffers from neglect, hmm?"

"Are you saying you want us to destroy you, Warlock?" I grunted.

"No, boy," Lucien said, "I'm trying to say that I've figured out just how we're related, my boy? Would you like to hear?"

"Shoot."

"Charlie, you know that we're mirror images, right now. But that's not where it stops. I am every iteration of you that will be and every version that has already been. Together, we are the Mists eating away at poor Vespa's heart as she dreams. You make the Mist that tells her sweet Lies and brings her blissful slumber. You fill her with hope and love. I birth the Mist that obscures the Truth and eats at her sanity. I want to see her hurt, writhing in agony. It's simple, really. Charlie, you are the yin to my yang, the zig to my zag. I can't exist without you, just as you cannot exist without me."

"Really? And how did you deduce that?"

"Because we're both little more than the results of an overactive neuron in the slumbering head of that girl over there. We're dreams, Charlie. It's time for us to wake up."

"Oh, we'll see about that, you bastard." I picked up a fallen shard of stained glass and hobbled over to the crippled Were. "I think it's about time we performed our little experiment."

"Charlie!" Vespa cried. "No, don't do it!"

I was beyond her words; my hands were already in motion. I stabbed Lucien in the neck with the green triangle, pushing it in deeper while pulling across his throat. Viscous red sap drained from his body, trickling down the glass. The colors combined to create bittersweet sepia. With little more than a sputter of froth, Lucien ceased to exist.

"Oh, I really wish you hadn't done that, Charlie. I really wish you'd stopped."

"Excuse me? I came here for revenge, and I took it. Why should I have stopped?"

"Well, now the world is going to fall apart."

"What do you mean? That's preposterous. The worst thing that could happen is that I'll die, but I don't even feel a little bit hurt. Wait, why don't I feel hurt?"

"Literally, every piece of this planet is going to shake itself apart, down to its tiniest elements. Charlie, don't you get it? This whole place is part of me. The Island, the Winged, the Mists, all of them came from my thoughts, my desires. Even Downy and Lucien were a part of me. Everything in this place is made from the stuff of my dreams. You just destroyed a keystone in the structure of my dream, and now I must wake. This world will be destroyed!"

"So, what about me?" I asked, my heart near fractures. "Am I any different? When you wake, will I just disintegrate? Will I return to the fabric of your mind? That's bullshit. I'm as real as real can be. You can't deny my reality."

"No, I know you're as real as me," Vespa began to cry. "You should have a broken leg. You should have died when you killed Lucien. You felt his pain. I felt it, too. That connection was real, right? But you're connected even more powerfully to me. Trust me, stay with me! My will is keeping you safe here."

"Then just stop protecting me!" I yelled. "Let me vanish into the nothing from whence I came."

"No, Charlie!" Vespa cried. "I would never do that. I could never. You are the one Truth that I can follow. You are no Lie. Take my hand. Let us fly away together and find a new land. Trust in me, Charlie. I know we can do this, together.

241

Remember? We're not supposed to be apart any more."

A deep growl shook the ground. Reality was beginning to fray, tearing apart the edges of the world.

"Please! You must believe me, Charlie! We can make it through this! We'll find a safe haven and build a better life! I promise. I don't have to wake up, not yet."

The fortress walls began to rumble. They wouldn't stand much longer against the dreamscape vibrations. Vespa gazed at me with beggar's eyes. Her mouth twisted in angst as if she knew what was I was thinking.

I loved her. Of that, there was no question. All of my identity might have been built on a lie, a name she picked out of thin air, but my heart contained molten emotion for this whimsical woman. I wanted to be with her, but this world was not my home. I was a figment of Vespa's imagination and nothing more. I had no home.

What to do? What to do?

ALT

Vespa extended her hand, soft warm fingers begging to be grasped. I reached out to clasp her hand, and a shocking bolt fused our hands together. An immeasurable static force bound us everywhere our skin touched. For a moment, our arms became one, a beam of light connecting our inner worlds.

"Come," Vespa whispered, "Let's go home."

"Where are we going?" I asked. "What's going to happen when the world is destroyed?"

"Shhh," Vespa placed a finger to her lips. "You've earned your wings. Fly with me, Charlie."

She bent her legs as though she had an itch then sprang vertically with every ounce of her power. If our bodies hadn't fused, I would not have been able to hang on for the ride.

We raced toward the ceiling, dark masonry threatening to stop our escape. But as we zoomed upward, the eaves melted away. Brick by brick, the castle vanished back to the realms of Mist and imagination. As we flew higher, I looked down and saw the walls erasing as though a typhoon of null-void was raining upon them. We passed through the lowest clouds and flirted for a bit with the heavenly pillows.

Another jet upwards made the clouds fall away until they looked like miniature cauliflowers, drifting about the surface of a placid lake. Still, Vespa carried us higher and higher. Air grew colder and thinner. Breathing was more challenging than usual. The blue sphere below us shrank until it was less than a pinprick in the sky's bubble. Dark nothingness speckled with astral lights expanded in all directions.

At such a great height, it became impossible to tell at what speed we zoomed through the universe. I couldn't even guess whether or not we still moved, relativistically speaking. We wandered lost in an infinite wilderness.

"Vespa!" I shouted, my voice muffled by the lack of atmospheric particles. "Where are we going? Do you have any idea what you're doing?"

"Not a clue," she replied, voice as clear as dawn. "I'm looking for a place. I don't know what I'm looking for, exactly, but we'll know it when we find it."

"But, there's nothing here. Nothing at all. Just lots and lots of stars that are super far away."

"Silly boy, you just don't know where to look!" she said. She pointed at the space below us.

I glanced down to see us skirting the edge of a burning, blue sphere. Flames from its surface licked at us, hungry for a taste of our fleet feet.

"When did that get there?" I exclaimed. "We nearly crashed and burned!"

"I know, isn't it cool?"

"Quite the opposite!"

"Oh, Charlie, just trust me and hold on tight. I'll show you a million things even cooler than that."

And she did. We navigated more galaxies than heads on a hydra. We skirted an asteroid belt. We discovered the difference between orbs and spheres. We sketched out shapes in the void and discovered a new brand of geometry. We flitted between twin stars in a dual neutron system, before they melted together in hot fusion death. A solar orchestra converged to play us a heavenly symphony. The music built and built, never quite reaching a discernable climax. Joy himself composed the piece, accompanied by Wonder.

After a short eternity, the music subsided and Vespa took us to a quaint little sphere in the back corner of our own galaxy. It was a perfect bubble of liquid water. The place wasn't much to look at, nothing more than infinite permutations of shades of blue. As our feet touched the planet's surface, they the water turned to hard, ochre earth. The transformation spread between molecules until we stood on a small island. As the soil continued to spread underwater, all across the planet, Vespa turned her attention to the earth beneath her fee.

She dug her fingers deep into the ground, tilling the loamy earth. Everywhere her fingers touched, a verdant green began to bloom. Primeval plants evolved before our eyes, growing from sprouts to tiny shrubs to elegant canopies. I pissed into the water encircling our island and sparked another chain reaction. Animal life emerged from my primal stream. The beasts morphed with such gusto! Wimpy frogs shifted into elegant toads.

Dumb lizards learned how to fly. A circular world matured, weaving an intricate web as it grew around us.

With all our machinations set in motion, we began to explore the microcosms we'd constructed. An eternity was given to every creature, as we inspected its essence and quality. There was so much to see out in the world, we didn't even think to explore ourselves.

A massive red pine grew ill at over six millennia in age. Its core was cancerous, so Vespa and I carved out the tumor. In exchange, the arboreal spirit offered us a haven in its trunk. We accepted his generosity. With the tree's blessing, we shaped the tree's wood into our furniture. After all was completed, we had a table with benches, a bed, shelves, and counter space for cooking. The tree got nervous when we brought home plants for dinner, so we ate nothing but meat. All our clothes were made from skin.

Life went on peacefully for a long while, as Vespa and I fell even more deeply in love. During this time, I figured out the best way to fight Vespa's sorcery: just give into it. As her enchantments swept over me with regularity, I learned the flow of her magic. With enough practice, I could just enjoy the ride.

Eventually, she fell under my own brand of sorcery and we committed the most magical of acts, a sacred rite reserved for gods like us. That night we rode each other until our bodies broke, wracked wIth pains from muscles we'd never known. It happened again the next night, and the night after that. It happened again and again until it seemed like time itself had slowed to a crawl. Or maybe it sped up. It was hard to tell if we still traveled through it at all, relativistically speaking.

The fury of our love was so intense that we didn't even notice Vespa's pregnancy until she was fat with child. Lovemaking stopped only when she grew too wide to waddle. Then our first child was born.

We repeated this grand cycle, but with a secret accomplice in our midst. Irredeemably in love, we possessed each other every night, but the tiny hands of our ultimate creation held our days. We groomed his hair. We told him secrets. We fed him flesh. We taught him maths. We called him Hammond.

Hammond was soon joined by a sister, Cheri, and a brother, Downy, who never managed to get along. Twins Beverly and Quinn always stole each other's clothing, never content in their given skins. Mola would spend his days staring out over the ocean, rarely saying a word, but with a huge smile on his face. We created thirty-one spawn before we couldn't make any more. Each of them was a perfect child, in his own way. Individually, they were bratty punks, but together they made our family.

Life rolled on and our love grew unfalteringly. Every addition to our family multiplied the power our hearts. We were building a unique human circuit board with a single function: the amplification of love. It was a perpetual love device: more love was always released than was put into the machine, with no measurable loss.

Our happiness approached infinity, with no sadness to even compare it against. There came only happy days and happier days. Less happy days were few and far between.

And then, after all was said and done, we died.

Death wasn't fast, but it was mostly painless. The disease manifested in our legs. Vespa and I spent a lot of time laying in bed those days, speaking all the words we'd been holding inside. All the sweet-talking in the world wasn't going to postpone the inevitable; we'd both known that for a long time. Even so, we made love with our minds when our bodies became too weak.

By the end, even that simple act became too hard to handle. Instead, we just lay side-by-side, clasping hands. She squeezed mine hard, twice times in the middle of the night, just to say goodbye. Neither of us woke the next morning, but the world carried on, levied by the strength of Vespa's memory.

Our children danced and sang to celebrate our lives, never mourning for our passing.

In a perfect world, things would have gone a little something like that. Of course, the world is far from perfect.

DELETE

In reality, things went like this:

Vespa extended her hand, her warm pink fingers begging to be grasped. I reached out to connect, but my hand stopped halfway on its journey. Some sort of curse was bubbling up inside me, countering Vespa's spell of temptation. I had learned a trick of my own, at the worst possible time.

"No," I said. "I can't come with you. This is your home and I am just a guest. I feel like my welcome has worn out. I'm sorry, Vespa."

"Charlie, don't talk like that!" Vespa said, rushing forward to embrace me. "Come on! Let's jet among the sparkles in the sky. Let's explore the million wonders we have yet to see."

I stopped her rush, placing my hands on her shoulders. "No," was all I could manage to choke out. Without another word, I turned away and walked into the settling Mists.

I wandered for little more than a day before breaking into sunlight on the edge of the Ides Marsh. Having been through the Mists once, I was proficient at navigating their bleak landscapes back to the Island. I saw Thunderpuss grazing on some reeds in the Marsh. He didn't make any sign that he recognized me or even that he noticed my presence.

I retraced our party's steps back to the foot of the Azure Egress, back through the woods to the

249

falcon cemetery. Every other hour, I could feel the earth trembling beneath my footsteps. I never once looked behind me. I knew that everything I saw would be erased after I passed. Things would hold together as long as Vespa could keep them stable. She would tire soon and wake, as soon as she could let me go.

It was another day before I found myself on the shore of the crater lake, looking at the Colony Helmsdotter. It was safe, but appeared empty from the outside. I couldn't feel the presence of any of the strange friends I'd made inside its walls. The pyramid was silent, as though the Mist had claimed its inhabitants. I figured they were already deleted from this world and moved onward.

I followed the shore and walked through a long tunnel carved into the Ring. It proved a much simpler path through the barrier than traveling down a river, chased by a hungry Were-fish. By nightfall I found myself back at the rumbly orchard; by dawn I was standing on the beach, facing Hammond's hut. The great egress was outside, waiting to greet me.

"Welcome back, little racist. Harrumph!" Hammond opened the door to his shack, inviting me inside. "I was wondering when I would see you again."

"Don't you mean 'if'? You couldn't have known I was coming back to the shore. Could you?"

"Oh, you took a bit longer than I expected, but I knew you would be back. Everyone I send into the forest comes back, eventually. And, every time, they forget to bring me my rumblies! Harrumph! Did you at least bring my bowl back, this time?"

"I'm sorry," I said, "I lost it in the wilderness."

"Harrumph! I suppose I should have expected as much. It'll show up again, sooner or later. It always does. I probably don't even need to ask, but will you be needing any help building a raft or craft? I gathered some supplies, because I thought you might say yes."

As a team, we lashed together one hundred one pieces of driftwood to create a flimsy flotation device. As repayment, I slipped out of Vespa's father's clothes and gave them to Hammond. He happily dressed one of his stuffed mini-bears. I was happy, too. Somewhere along my return journey, the outfit had stopped fitting me so well. It was much too loose. With a wave and a push, my naked self embarked on a journey to explore the Ocean outside the Island.

And now, at story's end, I find myself caught up to the present. My raft has drifted for several days on the ocean's currents. I'm too weak to do anything but trust the flows. I hope they are leading me toward some respectable destination. If I'm lucky, I'll wind up in some adventure proving that everything I think to be absolute truth is in reality little more than the product of ocean madness. That all the ordeals I just faced were nothing more than fever dreams induced by dehydration.

In truth, I don't really care where I'm going. All that matters to me is that I'm moving, slowly but surely. It's impossible for me to know where I will be when Vespa finally wakes or what will happen to this world we had both grown to love. As far as I know, she's long gone. She's probably living her life in the waking realm as it always has been: without me. She is wandering a world as real to her now as this raft is to me.

Though, this place grows a lot less believable without her around to make it feel alive.

Then again, maybe she was never anything at all. It is possible that she was just a figment of my imagination and that the Island was all a part of my dream or, even, that I'm still asleep. No, no. I know that's crazy talk. The crusty salt in my nose is much too poignant for this to be my own dream. If it's anyone's dream, it's hers.

I sometimes see tiny penguins crossing the sky above my raft, hoping that I'm dead so they can feast and rest on their epic journey. So far, none of them have been pink, and none have said a word to me. I think they're upset that I'm not already tasty and rotten for them to easily digest. It's not like I'm fighting it. I'm just spinning, floating along, waiting for something to happen.

Sometimes, I wonder if the only reason I still exist is because she thinks of me, from time to time. When I'm on her mind, I'm awake and aware. When she's in her own world, I simply fade away. This whole place fades away. Maybe when she's awake, that's when I dream.

I do dream, every night when I sleep or vanish or whatever. It's always different. The hooded stranger still hasn't shown his face. I'm never in a precarious position. The only thing I can count on is that Vespa won't be there. Her absence in my dreamscapes is duly noted.

A sick fantasy fills the moments after I wake. I hope that maybe I still have a purpose. Maybe, someday, I'll be called back into Vespa's life. She might choose to abandon her current reality and give me another chance. She might yet crawl back inside her fantasyland and beckon me back to the shore. I know these are dangerous thoughts. The more hope I wear as armor, the deeper I'll sink when the raft capsizes. I know the risks, but I can't chain down my own hope. It's inhumane.

It is all I can do to record this journey, tracing my thoughts into the water with a lazy finger. Some fish or aquatic deity or manatee might understand what I mean to get across. Maybe they can explain to me what I mean. At the very least, I hope someone will listen. That hope lays me on my back and tells me to look up at the sky, unfettered by clouds. A hot breeze whisks away my inhibitions as I stare into the sun. I pray to the omnipotent guardians of heaven and hell to not let me vanish into oblivion. Asking for someone's ear when you don't even know their name is sort of awkward and stressful. Despite it all, I feel better. Some ghost in the world beyond this one is surely listening to my prayers. Surely.

A leviathan wave creeps towards my rocking bed. It is a blanket placed upon me by an invisible mother's love. It tucks me in, wrapping my body tight in its moist embrace. The raft and I are pulled deeper and deeper by its seductive undertow.

I glance up one last time at the surface, knowing full well I will never rise again. The sun marks a gleaming circle, of blinding flashes. It winks at me once, and I see a familiar face among the ripples. I force a smile as the accumulating pressure pushes the last gulp of air from my lungs. My prayers are answered. I am not forgotten.

Sun-scorched and well cured, I wake on an unfamiliar shore, under unfamiliar skies. My senses are flooded by uncertainty. I wouldn't bet a dollar as to which grainy beach I have washed onto, let alone who I am supposed to be. The salty ocean waters have smoothed my mind like a pebble and only a well-worn sense of self remains.

And yet, as the hot, pink sun beats relentlessly on my naked body, I know that I am home.

ABOUT THE AUTHOR

Samuel Sobelman lives in heart of the Irvine Corporation with his beard (Schmooley), cactus (Señor), and his bicycle (Pantalaimon). He spends his time typing away, strumming his guitar, trimming back his mustache (Octavius), and doing all sorts of chemistry-related things. He often plays in a band with Madeline (Lauren) Browning, artist extraordinaire. Together, they are Captain Macaque and the Wire Mothers.

Sam has written one previous novel: *AlphaBetaPocalypse.* If you enjoyed this book, you should probably check that out, too. You know, whenever you get around to it.

Visit www.samsobelman.com for music downloads, short stories, and previews of Sam's works to come.

This is the end of Sam's second novel.

www.ingramcontent.com/pod-product-compliance
Lightning Source LLC
Chambersburg PA
CBHW071136170626
46809CB00002B/643